Shuttered Windows

Books by
FLORENCE CRANNELL MEANS

PENNY FOR LUCK

A BOWLFUL OF STARS

A CANDLE IN THE MIST

RANCH AND RING

DUSKY DAY

TANGLED WATERS

THE SINGING WOOD

SHUTTERED WINDOWS

ADELLA MARY IN OLD NEW MEXICO

AT THE END OF NOWHERE

WHISPERING GIRL

SHADOW OVER WIDE RUIN

TERESITA OF THE VALLEY

THE MOVED-OUTERS

HARRIET

Shuttered Windows

By

Florence (Crannell) Means, 1891-

Illustrations by
ARMSTRONG SPERRY

HOUGHTON MIFFLIN COMPANY · BOSTON
The Riverside Press Cambridge

The Riverside Press
CAMBRIDGE · MASSACHUSETTS
PRINTED IN THE U.S.A.

TO

MATHER SCHOOL

THIS SMALL SHADOW OF ITSELF IS

GRATEFULLY DEDICATED

CONTENTS

CONTENTS

ILLUSTRATIONS

I

GRANDFATHER MOSES

HARRIET curled up in the back seat of the car with her foot asleep and did not say a word for miles and miles.

She was usually talkative enough. Today there were good reasons for her silence. Mr. Trindle, behind the steering wheel, gave no one else a chance to slip in a word edgewise; the fifteen hundred miles between Minneapolis, Minnesota, and Charleston, South Carolina, had exhausted her vocabulary; she was soon to meet an unknown great-grandmother who was her only kin, and on the way to that great-grandmother's home visit the boarding-school where she might enroll for her senior year. In addition to all this novelty, there was Moses to hold her speechless.

Moses emerged from dim woods paths. Down the dark aisles of cypress swamps, between the swaying pennons of Spanish moss, he rowed with a rhythm of mighty shoulders. Through the sweet gum and the feathery mimosa that skirted the highway he strode with a rhythm of mighty legs.

If he disappeared like a puff of smoke in the misty mosses or on the winding paths, that was not strange:

Moses was Harriet's great-great-great-grandfather. She had always dreamed of him with fierce pride, an ancestor to boast of; but never had she seen him so clearly as now, when for the first time she came into his own place.

So she sat in the back seat, well packed about with blankets and cushions, and looked from side to side. Mr. Trindle discoursed steadily upon the rich history of the Charleston district, and Mrs. Trindle broke his flow of conversation with an occasional 'Tk! Tk!' at sight of a cart drawn by a lumbering ox, or a woman with a reed basket balanced on her head, or a vast live-oak bearded with moss. Sometimes Mr. Trindle's discourse faltered while he mopped his brow and neck and shining, beaded dome. Sometimes, but not often, Mr. Trindle paused for breath.

Unconsciously Harriet filled in those rare pauses with a phrase of song, hummed in a lilting, birdlike voice, or with a wriggle and chuckle of delight. If she could have had Helen and Iva and Jimmie with her, the experience would have been perfect. But letters were so stupid: they could never capture the sight and smell and feel of the South for the 'gang' in Minneapolis.

The distance from Minneapolis to Charleston was so much more than the fifteen hundred miles the dizzy, diagonal figures on their touring map indicated: it stretched from the world of Harriet, today, back to the world of Moses, 1836.

Here was the Ford, to be sure, and her own modern fitted traveling case at her feet. Here were other cars meeting theirs, passing it, in endless current along the smooth pavement. But — here were tall cypress trees, their silver knees rising from ink-black waters. Here were villages whose weathered, gray cabins had sat down to sleep in the forest wherever they happened to. Here were batten doors, and rude shutters swinging at glassless window places, and enormous black kettles steaming over fires that smouldered on the ground.

Now and then the car flashed past a Big House straight out of a Civil War romance, its tall pillars cutting lovely white lines from ground to roof; and Charleston, behind them now, had been rich in gracious dwellings roofed with mossy tiles and flowering into ancient iron grill-work.

Somewhere in this region Taliaferro Plantation had stood in just such gracious beauty: Taliaferro, where Moses had had his being. So it was natural that Harriet should see him here.

Legend had sprung up about Moses, but the fact that it was legend made her no less proud. Even when she was small, her father had said: 'Honey-child reverts to type, Mother. Mark my word, she gets her height from Grandpa Moses; those broad little old shoulders, too, and the uppity way she flings back her head.'

Harriet liked to recall the words, with the rich laugh chuckling through them. She liked to remember all she could of the home that for a while had been so happy and complete.

After Father's death came four years when Harriet's mother served as Y.W.C.A. secretary, as she had done before her marriage: Four years in a small, bright apartment, where Harriet practised and played and grew into lanky girlhood. A year ago the small, bright apartment had been dismantled, and Harriet had gone to live with Mr. and Mrs. Trindle, a motherless as well as a fatherless girl.

Mr. Trindle had long been the pastor of their church and their friend. His house was a home, rich in books and magazines and dog-eared music and a piano shabby from the practising of Trindle children now grown and away. It was as pleasant as an adoptive home could be. The insurance her mother had left took care of Harriet's small needs, though the warm fathering and mothering hearts of the Trindles would not have left her unprovided for in any case. Yet Harriet was not happy. After months of wild grieving, she had tried to settle down in her new nest, but she did not succeed very well. She felt like a visitor who must soon go on to her own home and her own people.

So far as she knew, her 'own people' numbered exactly one; her father's grandmother, living on what Harriet thought of as the old homestead, far in the mysterious deeps of the South.

Great-Grandmother was mysterious, too. Father could barely remember her, for he had been brought North in his early childhood. Every Christmas a festive box of gifts had gone to Gentlemen's Island. Other than that, there had been no communication with her. Great-Grandmother must be very old, Harriet thought; and very old people, with shaky hands and failing sight, did not often write.

Even Harriet's letter, written a few weeks after her mother's death, had not been answered by Great-Grandmother herself. She had replied by the hand of one 'R. Corwin.'

R. Corwin wrote on stationery that had evidently aged in a village store: it held definite flavors of tobacco and drugs and dried fish and perfume and kerosene. On the stale paper, in somewhat stiff phrases, R. Corwin had expressed Great-Grandmother's sympathy, and her affectionate desire to see her only living descendant.

'Your Granny,' R. Corwin had written, 'begs you will come and pay her a visit; but her deepest wish is that you live here. She says tell you there is always room in her house for you. Also there is a fine girls' school on a near island. You must have heard of it. Landers is its

4

name, and girls in these parts have been educated there since the War Between the States. An old school and very honorable.

'Perhaps it is not right that I should tell you, but your Granny prays even in the meeting-house that her child shall come home to her before she dies. She is a respected woman: good, also very smart.'

Harriet handed that letter to Mr. and Mrs. Trindle and watched them read it. Mr. Trindle's scraggly eyebrows arched above the gold rims of his spectacles, and Mrs. Trindle clucked softly. With simultaneous question they looked at Harriet. Harriet, knitting her brows as she did when she felt strongly, answered with decision: 'I'd like to go. Maybe for a year.'

Mr. Trindle pushed out his lips and tapped them with the folded letter. 'Slowly, slowly, my child. What would be the effect of such a venture on the progress of your musical education?'

Harriet touched the piano with an unconscious hand. She was accompanist for the glee club in the big high school and was achieving a modest fame in her world. Besides, the past year had taught her to love music for its own sake. But her head went back in the 'uppity way' Father had noticed long ago. 'If my music's any good, a little interruption won't hurt it. And a great-grandmother all alone ——'

Mrs. Trindle looked past Harriet out of the window and her eyes narrowed and widened, narrowed and widened. 'What about your chums, Harrie? I don't reckon it would be so easy to pick up congenial friends ——'

Helen and Iva. Yes, and Jimmie, too. 'But a great-grandmother ought to count more than the kids you go round with.'

'Papa,' said Mrs. Trindle, with the double blink that meant that her words were a sort of code, 'don't you

want to come out and open a jar for me? Seems like I
haven't the strength ——'

Harriet heard them in the kitchen, Mrs. Trindle's coo
answered by Mr. Trindle's astonished rumble; the coo
again; the rumble, grown calmer; silences broken by coo
and rumble. At the dinner table Mr. Trindle portentously
cleared his throat and informed Harriet that he and Mrs.
Trindle had always had the most intense desire to motor
to the Deep South for their vacation.

So, when summer was waning toward autumn, the
three went whirring through the country in the swift
comfort of a new, gray Ford. They stopped in New York,
in Washington, in Charleston. Now they were drawing
near Bosquet and Landers School; drawing near Gentlemen's Island and Great-Grandmother.

Now, too, the ancestor Moses assumed more and more
reality: a mighty man with the nobly held head of lofty
birth. Some had said he was the son of a Mohammedan
priest; some, the son of a petty king. Certain it was that
he had survived the terrible Middle Passage to become
a slave with other slaves on a South Carolina rice plantation.

With what satisfaction he would have regarded this
descendant of his, whose head was unbowed in the land
of his captivity! Harriet was as handsome as he could
have been: a bronze maiden, eyes straight-gazing under
brows that frowned with thought; hair cloudy black; full
lips well cut; smooth, brown skin stained with dusky red.

A child of Moses — of Black Moses.

It was not until the car passed over the causeways that
led across reedy waters to the old city of Bosquet that
Harriet's thoughts for a little while ceased to swing between Great-Grandmother and Moses, and settled down
to Landers School. The school must be their first stop,
for its opening day was close upon them.

They had visited a school in Charleston, one whose pupils were called the 'colored aristocracy.' White people might laugh at the term, but it was not ludicrous: these girls and boys were the flower of generations of educated people.

But it was on Landers that Harriet had set her heart, not only because it was nearer Great-Grandmother, but because she liked the sound of it. 'An old school and very honorable,' R. Corwin had said; and 'girls in these parts have been educated there since the War Between the States.'

Seventy years! That was venerable to the girl from the Middle West. Her own high school was beautiful: endless, shining corridors; mellow woods; statues white in dim corners; a library with Gothic windows and easy study chairs and book-tapestried walls. Beautiful; but so new!

'Bosquet,' Mr. Trindle was going on with relish, 'is historically remarkable. The region hereabout is marked by some of the earliest landings on the continent. The Spanish landed in 1520 and the French Huguenot, Jean Ribaut, in 1560 or thereabouts. And within the confines of Bosquet itself, if I mistake not, exists a church edifice that dates from 1720.'

Mrs. Trindle, a plump and cozy brown pigeon of a woman, was tk-tking constantly now, for they were bowling along through the dusty, narrow streets of the town. Here more of the stately Big Houses paraded the waterfront; blossoming shrubs and garden flowers splashed the scene with color; and in the midst of the residences stood ruined, gray masonry with wrought-iron banisters leading upward to nothing, and flowers and thick leafage thrusting through the breaches everywhere. The city looked as if it had slept, charmingly, since 1864.

Harriet screwed sidewise to look out the back window

7

at some long buildings on the end of shadowy old grounds.

'Mr. Trindle,' she asked, 'what would those be for? With funny little high windows barred like a jail?'

Mrs. Trindle made a mournful noise, and Mr. Trindle cleared his throat. 'Slave quarters, Harrie,' he answered, handling the word gingerly, as one touches a tender scar. 'Just observe the brick wall surrounding this ancient church. Green with moss and mould. Doubtless the edifice to which I referred: 1720.'

Harriet winced, and turned her eyes from those barred windows to the old church and the old street.

More Negroes than white people walked the street: laughing, playing, quarreling children; grown people; old men, bent and shuffling; old women, peering from below white headcloths. Harriet studied the old women with her heart in her mouth. Her great-grandmother would not be like these. Harriet wanted to hurry to that meeting, and at the same time she flinched from it. She was both eager and afraid. She had not realized how different might be Harriet-of-South Carolina from Harriet-of-Minnesota.

First, however, it was necessary to visit Landers School.

Mr. Trindle inquired the way, and drove along the ribbon of black pavement that was pointed out to him.

The highway became the dark floor of a tunnel, walled and roofed with green and draped with gray. When Mr. Trindle had whizzed through the tunnel a while, he brought the car to a squealing stop, backed a little, and parked behind a trim, tan cousin Ford, with a South Carolina license. Over an aisle opening into the deep green an arched sign announced LANDERS SCHOOL.

Harriet felt herself gathered up into a tight ball of excitement as she jumped from the car and walked along the aisle with Mr. and Mrs. Trindle. This was one of Life's Moments! Who knew to what experiences this brief walk would carry her? Nothing else holds out such promises as a new school: new surroundings, new friends, new teachers, and one's self somehow a new person. Harriet surreptitiously twitched her sheer cotton dress straight and pulled her hat properly over one eye.

She had a momentary glimpse of a campus shaded by great trees; of a flame of flowers. Then her attention went to a group of people who stood facing back, apparently, toward buildings they had just left.

The people were of the type she had seen on the dusty roads, fishing in little creeks or trudging along with burdens on their heads or slung over their shoulders. The women wore the characteristic headcloths and gold hoop earrings. The man's hat was almost crownless. They were laughing and talking to each other, their voices deep and throaty.

'—— jis' gran', enty?' murmured one. 'Ever I yeddy how gran' e was.'

'But never did I reckon my chillen gwine live like white folks,' said another, her voice splitting on a note of pure awe. 'E *too* pretty, enty?'

They became aware of the Trindle group, and edged aside to let them pass, grinning and bowing and blinking curious eyes at them. Mrs. Trindle nudged Harriet along, for the girl unconsciously slowed her steps to listen. Here was a strange language, not only softly slurred, but pieced together with extra syllables — 'Nevah did Ah reckon ma chillen duh-gwan lib lak duh whi' folks' — and with strange words: 'enty,' 'yeddy.' It was as lovely as French patois. Harriet wanted to hear more.

But, urged past the trio, she looked eagerly for the grandeur that had awed them. White temples of learning, maybe, with pillared façades gleaming out of green glooms.

Another couple passed, bowing. Harriet thought idly that they were headed for the tan Ford on the highway.

The woman wore crisp white, and the man a Panama at one end and white buckskin shoes at the other: an ordinary, uninterestingly well-dressed colored man and woman.

Harriet's eyes passed them while she returned their bows; and quite suddenly she was looking at the words OFFICE above the door of a square wooden house.

They entered. Harriet felt herself falling through her bright imaginings and landing with a jolt on reality. No shining corridors here; no mellow woods and Gothic windows; instead, a splintery, scrubbed floor and plain board walls that could have made good use of a fresh coat of paint; and a shabby desk across which a serene-faced woman smiled at them.

'May I help you in some way?' asked the serene-faced woman. 'I am Miss Francis, the Principal of Landers.'

Dizzy from her bump on reality, Harriet stared at Miss Francis's pale face and honey-colored hair. The principal's lips did not smile, but her blue eyes did.

'Permit me to present Mrs. Trindle,' Mr. Trindle was enunciating deeply, 'and our young friend Miss Harriet Freeman. Of Minneapolis, Minnesota.' He drew out a card-case and laid his card on the desk.

Harriet was looking about her, still with a floating feeling as if she were dreaming the whole scene. On a bulletin board was pinned a notice headed: THE SENIORS AIM TO PLEASE. And lettered below was the information:

All are Workers in the Senior Hive.
We polish Shoes while you wait: 5¢ a Pair.
We make Dresses: 50¢ if not too fancy.
Also collars and nightgowns.

Patronize our Beauty Shop.
Hair straightened and curled.
We improve you 100%.

The Senior Class. That would be her class. That would *have been* her class, she corrected herself vigorously. For the dullest person could see that it would not be good sense for her to give up Centennial High and Minneapolis for Landers and South Carolina.

Noticing her intent gaze, the principal turned to her from her conversation with the Trindles. 'Every class earns money for a party and a present,' she explained. 'That is last year's bulletin. Those seniors were an energetic group. They'd do anything to earn a dollar.'

Harriet moistened her lips. 'Does it really mean — could they make a dress for fifty cents?'

'"If not too fancy." Fifty cents isn't so small a coin here as it is up North,' Miss Francis answered, her eyes warming with their unexpected smile. 'When you consider how low our fees are, at Landers, and board ——

'But wouldn't you like to see our buildings? I'll show you our newest first. Sarah B. Lawrence. We're proud of it.'

She led the way to a long brick edifice with a pillared entrance. At sight of it Harriet felt more at ease: it was not utterly different from her expectations. Downstairs were dining-rooms and living-rooms; upstairs, rows and rows of small bedrooms. The principal glowed over them, her look broodingly content, and Harriet scrutinized the plain little rooms, wondering what there was about them to make anyone so happy.

Miss Francis swayed down the corridors, tall, slender, her head bent a little to one side on her long throat. Mr. Trindle strode after her with the swing of the small man, and Mrs. Trindle pattered by his side; you almost expected her shoes to be pink, like pigeons' feet. Both Trindles made polite remarks at appropriate moments, while their faces remained blank.

'Miss Harriet would naturally be assigned to this

pleasantest dormitory,' Miss Francis explained. 'It is the upper-class hall. But it is already completely filled by the advance applications. There is, of course, always the possibility of a cancellation.'

She ushered them out and across the campus toward the other buildings, telling about fees as she went. Registration was eight dollars, board eighty-one dollars for the year, high-school books about eight dollars, music lessons two dollars a month. Harriet kept trying to figure the total, but she could never get past two times eight is sixteen, plus eighty-one is — There her mind would falter and leap to the music lessons at two dollars a month. In Minneapolis she paid two dollars for a half-hour.

Miss Francis was explaining that the students all did some housework, caring for their own rooms and corridors and taking turns waiting on tables. She broke off to usher them into a barnlike three-story house.

'This is the middle dormitory, Washington Hall. It was built shortly after the Civil War, out of lumber from Union barracks.' At the opening of the door a musty, salt-sweet odor had encompassed them, as if seventy years had made a strange potpourri. The steep stairs creaked warningly as they climbed; the hall floor creaked as they paced its length, looking into the tiny rooms.

Now Harriet understood Miss Francis's pride in Sarah B. Lawrence. Each of these Washington cubicles had space for two cot beds, a curious iron washstand that grasped in iron loops a wash basin and pitcher, and a stove like an enlarged shoe-box on legs. Across two corners curtains formed triangular clothes closets.

'You've probably noticed that none of our walls are papered,' Miss Francis observed cheerfully. 'It's too damp here: paper peels off at once.'

Harriet looked mutely at the painted wood. She was finding Mr. Trindle's steady stream of talk more agreeable than usual. He filled all conversational space, and wherever there was a hole Mrs. Trindle dropped in a word. Harriet did not have to hunt things to say. Her direct mind balked at polite untruths. She was glad she need only walk beside the others and see the buildings as they were displayed.

She saw the shabby schoolrooms and the library with its plain wooden tables for study and its miscellaneous books. She saw the cooking laboratory, with its hollow square of zinc-covered tables and its small gasoline stoves. 'The individual stoves aren't usable at present,' Miss Francis regretted, 'but it's really better for the girls to use the wood stove anyway; few of them have ever used any kind of gas; many of them probably never will.'

Harriet saw the industrial building — Jaynes Hall — one of the few new brick buildings on the campus. It held ranks of laundry tubs and files of ironing boards and stoves like old-fashioned heaters, with shelves around their sides on which clean black flatirons stood with their heating surfaces pressed against the clean, black stove walls and their handles out like ornamental curlicues.

Still dazed, she walked back to the office.

'Mrs. Trindle and Miss Harriet and myself are about to embark for Gentlemen's Island,' Mr. Trindle was rolling along in his pleasant, pompous voice. 'We shall take the matter under advisement and bring our young friend in by the opening date' — he brought his glasses to bear on the catalogue in his hand — 'the ninth, if we decide that it is advisable. I observe that the meteorologists are warning us of a West Indian hurricane heading toward the Florida Keys. Let us hope that this coast will escape such a visitation.' He was tapering off the interview with polite talk.

'I hope — I really hope Miss Harriet will decide to come to us,' Miss Francis said, for a moment holding

Harriet's baffled brown gaze with her intent blue one.
Miss Francis was as direct as Harriet. She hadn't even
noticed Mr. Trindle's tactful remarks.

'Will decide! Hmph! As if I hadn't already decided!'
Harriet was thinking, while she murmured and Mrs.
Trindle cooed and Mr. Trindle uttered sounding phrases,
and all three bowed themselves away and walked through
the shadowy aisle to the black highway.

Mr. Trindle started the car. 'Conditions differ greatly
in different sections of the country,' he observed pleasantly.

'Good gracious!' agreed Harriet. She looked at Mrs.
Trindle under drawn brows. 'What on earth did those
people mean, calling it grand, Mrs. Trindle?'

Mrs. Trindle clucked and lifted her plump little
shoulders. 'I'm beginning to think we have no idea of the
sectional differences, Harrie — no idea!'

Harriet was riffling the catalogue pages. 'Listen to
this,' she gurgled, and read aloud with slow weight:
'"Correspondence with young men is allowed to high-
school girls if parents send to the office names of those
whom they approve of. Each high-school girl may write
three letters each Monday." Can you imagine what Helen
and Iva would say to that?'

'Southern customs — Maybe conditions make closer
supervision necessary, Harrie — We may meet other
surprises, too.'

Great-Grandmother: that was what Mrs. Trindle was
warning her about. Harriet felt a sick churning in the
middle of herself. What on earth would Great-Grandmother be like?

II

GREAT-GRANDMOTHER

A MILE away at the Bosquet wharf the boat was already tootling. Mr. Trindle drove quickly back to town and left the car in a garage, and the three hurried down where the business buildings backed onto the creaky old dock. With expectancy tightening every nerve, Harriet followed Mrs. Trindle across the gangplank and up a stairway to the next deck. Here shabbily dressed Negroes were shouting and laughing to each other, or beginning to eat lunches out of shoe-boxes and paper bags.

'There's more room on top. Let's go up there,' said Harriet, pushing toward another staircase.

Mrs. Trindle laid a hand on her arm. 'No, Harrie. That's not for us. That's the white people's deck. This — Look, honey!'

Harriet's frowning gaze followed Mrs. Trindle's pointing finger. Over the door of the enclosed deck was a large sign: COLORED. Over the staircase she had wished to climb stood a similar sign: WHITE.

Harriet sat down, feeling sick. She had of course read of the 'Jim Crow' trains and waiting-rooms, but it was the first time she had ever encountered them herself.

'Let us go out into the fresh air and sunshine,' Mr. Trindle suggested, his eyes gleaming with comprehension behind his bright glasses. Harriet followed limply.

It was impossible to remain limp, perched on a bench in the bow. Harriet took off her hat. The breeze blowing in her face cool from the water flattened her lashes and twitched at her hair and blew every curling tendril straight back. The sun struck sparks from the water and gulls called and wheeled around the boat and the foam curled up before them and swished away behind them. Even the sea smell of salt and fish and iodine was intoxicating. Harriet's spirits flew up, light as a gull. She tossed back her head and laughed aloud.

Mr. and Mrs. Trindle laughed, too. 'It certainly does make an individual thankful for the gift of life,' said Mr. Trindle, the gold fillings in his teeth and the gold rims on his glasses vying with each other in the sunshine.

They passed small, slumbrous islands where old houses dreamed among palmettos and live-oaks: islands shut off from the world because they had no landing places. An occasional clumsy rowboat that had put off from a marshy shore awaited the steamer in midchannel, and stood by while a passenger climbed over the rail; then, with long pulls of the oars, nosed in among the rushes again.

Harriet drummed on the bench with her strong musician's fingers and thought that some day she would make music that would carry this swish and fury of waters, and cry of birds, and insistent fluting of the whistle.

Mrs. Trindle brought out the box of food which she had provided, and Harriet's thoughts surged from music to eating.

'Mmmm!' she murmured contentedly, 'an ocean voyage gives you an appetite!'

She buttered buns; and Mr. Trindle opened a can of sardines, holding it out over the railing as he twisted the key that rolled back the top flap; and Mrs. Trindle slipped two silvery fish into each bun and laid a bun and two fig-bars and a banana on a paper napkin on each lap. From somewhere Mr. Trindle summoned a pop boy, and opened three root-beer and orange-crush bottles with enticing spurts of foam. They ate and drank with deep relish.

When she was done, Harriet wadded her napkin around her banana peel and tried to toss it out over the rail. Perversely it blew back and down. She heard a shout of laughter from the lower deck and peered over into the upturned face of a boy who grinned and waved the pink napkin as if it had been a rose.

She could not help laughing back, though he was one of those swaggering, assured boys whom she liked to snub. He had a dimple in one cheek, as if someone had screwed a fingertip around in it, and his teeth gleamed like new ivory. He twisted a corner of the napkin into a stem and stuck it behind his ear and thrummed an imaginary guitar. The banana trailed down out of the crumpled pinkness, so that Harriet and Mr. and Mrs. Trindle all laughed again, leaning over the rail.

But then, much too soon, the boat ride was over. The whistle uttered long pipings, and the three travelers straightened and looked ahead. The steamer was chugging up to the barnacle-crusted stilts of a dock; chugging up pompously while the water churned against its sides and surged away and back again.

This was Great-Grandmother's island.

Mr. and Mrs. Trindle and Harriet stood amid their luggage on the clattering dock and watched the flurry of landing. A few Negroes had lounged out of the COLORED deck with them, laughing and shouting to others who laughed and shouted from the shore. A few pieces of freight had been landed, with yells and laughter. Harriet

17

watched absorbedly as four Negroes, their bodies glistening wet and brown through ragged denim, made a living
chain down a cleated slope to the freight deck and dragged
huge cakes of ice up to the pier. One clasped another to
form the chain, the last one grappled the ice, and all together climbed the cleated slope, dragging the burden.

On the shore two little colored boys in ragged overalls
ran along the beach picking up shells. A white man in a
white suit glanced indifferently at the Trindles and got
into his car and puffed back through the sand.

Mr. Trindle hailed a Negro with a brimless felt hat
perched on the side of his head. The man grinned at him
in friendly fashion. 'Brother,' asked Mr. Trindle, 'are
there any taxicabs operating in this vicinity?'

The man took off his hat and scratched his head.
'Which?'

· 'Any automobile we can engage to convey us to Sister
Freeman's home? Are you acquainted with a lady by the
name of Freeman?'

'Sho'. Mis' Freeman,' the man said, replacing the hat
he had removed to scratch his head. 'Ain' no automobiles
fuh hire, but I reckon y'all can walk it. Mis' Freeman
ain' live such a far piece. Y'all just follow thisyere road
to the fork and go to the right twell y'all done pass a
cane patch. House nex' the cane patch is blue. That
Mis' Freeman's.'

'Whoosh!' said Mr. Trindle, after they had trudged
along for ten minutes without sighting the fork. It was
heavily hot, here on the island. Mr. Trindle plumped the
three suitcases down in the dust, and swung his thin
brown neck in a half-circle while he wiped it with a damp
handkerchief. His collar was a white rag that had long
given up the effort to stand.

Harriet, roused by the ejaculation, caught up her own
suitcase self-reproachfully. She had not even noticed that

Mr. Trindle was laboring along with the heavy luggage while she and Mrs. Trindle carried only their overnight cases. She was scarcely aware of the afternoon sultriness, and of the way the 'piece' had stretched on through minutes muffled in deep, white dust. As one held in an enchantment, she tramped on toward her only living kin.

The island was held in enchantment, too. All the charm, the sleepy antiquity, that she had seen scattered along the way from Washington to Bosquet were boiled down in this small island ringed round by palms and rushes and waves.

The whole place seemed asleep. One automobile passed them, and Mr. Trindle turned toward it a hopeful brown face, glistening with sweat, but it was a white people's car and passed without a sign. Horses jogged by, bestridden by ragged boys and men. A vehicle creaked up behind them, wheels squalling. Harriet's attention was fixed on a thicket of palmetto where a mocking-bird did a wild dance of song, and she was dreamily considering that the bird would form the motif for another composition, with its sweet full calls and its pixy variations, whimsical, peevish. She did not turn to see the complaining cart until a great horned head appeared at her elbow. She leaped aside into the weeds, the suitcase banging her knees and the prickers snagging her stockings. A piebald ox swayed by between sapling thills. The rude two-wheeled cart he pulled was heaped with long rods like purple fishpoles, and topped by assorted human beings.

The cart screeched to a stop. The driver, his back bowed, his forearms on his knees, asked, 'Cain' I tote yo' satchels, Mister?'

Mr. Trindle nodded gratefully and heaved the large ones up among the purple sticks, wheezing, 'Sister Freeman's, thank you.'

'Sho'! Mis' Freeman's,' the man said, and nodded. The

cart groaned onward again, and the little old granny in the back end nodded and grinned at them around her little black pipe, and lifted a gnarled black hand in farewell.

The cart had scarcely disappeared to the right, where the road forked, when a still more startling interruption occurred. With a crash of underbrush and a rustle of weeds a beast hurtled out of a thicket and careened onto the road, where it skidded to a stop, flinging up its heels almost in Harriet's face.

'Now-now-now-now, young one! Mind where you're going, please!' Mr. Trindle adjured the apparition.

The calf was ridden by an imp with bare arms and legs like brown wires. This imp stared back at them over her shoulder and her grin displayed a startling gap in her front teeth.

'Oooh — Lawzy!' she whooped, and clapping her hands to her mouth and her heels into the calf's sides, she was off in a scramble of hoofs and tasseled tail and rocking-horse motion fore and aft.

'Good gracious!' Harriet cried, thoroughly awake. 'If this isn't the weirdest place! Ox carts full of purple fish-poles, and imps riding calves — and whole fields of white roses.'

Mr. Trindle cackled. 'That field's not flowers, Harrie: it's cotton. And your fishing-rods were sugar cane.'

'I don't know whether I can endure another step,' Mrs. Trindle panted. 'These new shoes have made a blister on my heel — I didn't know we'd have to walk across whole islands — and I'm about to melt and run away besides. Can't we go and sit on that porch a minute?' Her round face was slick with sweat.

'Oh, but it's such a dreadful shack,' Harriet objected. 'I know it's picturesque, but — Don't you suppose that cornfield-looking place ahead is the cane patch the man told us about? With Great-Grandmother's house just beyond it?'

'Well — ' Mrs. Trindle's eyes fastened hopefully on the light silken shimmer of green, while she spread her toes and wriggled the heel of her shoe loose. A trickle of perspiration zigzagged down her nose.

Mr. Trindle contemplated the despised shack. '"The young folk roll on the little cabin floor,"' he sang wheezily. 'Reckon that is precisely the type of domicile to which the song writer had reference.'

As they approached the cane patch the imp on the steer dashed toward them again, swerved her bucking steed to one side, and rocked back.

'You don't reckon it's a reception committee, do you?' Mrs. Trindle took breath to wonder.

'Mrs. Trindle, I think you have hit the nail on the head with your customary accuracy,' said Mr. Trindle.

Harriet had eyes for nothing but the farther boundary of the cane patch. She was watching for the blue house, the only home in all the world that was really hers. Reaching the far corner of the green silk field, she jerked to a standstill and stared.

Like the shack they had just passed, except that this was bluewashed instead of whitewashed, Great-Grandmother's home sat back at the edge of the thicket and waited for them. And at the door, standing bent yet tall —

With a murmured 'Excuse me!' Harriet ran ahead of Mr. and Mrs. Trindle, in at the gate, up the path, across the rickety porch. Great-Grandmother was holding her off with big, trembling hands, and gazing at her with wet old eyes on a level with her own. Great-Grandmother was folding her close, against a white kerchief that smelled of soap and sun. Great-Grandmother was crooning huskily, 'My own li'l gran'!'

In a moment she was recovering her poise and bowing to the Trindles. 'Y'all come a far piece!' she said politely. 'I'm right glad fuh see you. Come in. Come in an' res' yo' hats.'

The imp appeared, surprisingly divested of her steer, seized their hats and bags, and deposited them on the bed, at whose foot already stood the suitcases that had gone on ahead. Soon Mrs. Trindle was swaying in the single old rocking-chair and chirping about the orange and brown velvet marigolds she could see through the open door, and Mr. Trindle was easing his trousers over his knees and sitting down on a stool and clearing his throat and asking the imp, 'And who might this young lady be?'

The imp, sheltering herself behind Great-Grandmother, squirmed as if she were going through setting-up exercises and inspected her hands as if they were brand new. Great-Grandmother dragged her forth with a large kindliness. 'Lily, ain' I tol' you-all to be mannersable to ladies and gentlemen? — E's de drift dat lives wid me, suh.'

'*Drift?*'

'Yessuh. No fader, no mudder, no home. Just a li'l drift.'

Harriet's eyes and brain were clearing and steadying. She was in the cleanest of cabin sitting-rooms. Its walls and ceiling, its doors and shutters, were tidily papered with fresh magazine and newspaper pages. The doors and windows were curtained with white cheesecloth, which blew out lazily because there was no glass. The uneven floor was gay with rag rugs, and a neatly quilt-covered bed filled a quarter of the floor space.

And Great-Grandmother? She sat on a stool before the fireplace, the drift between her knees staring goblinlike at the company. Granny, in a patched calico dress and a white kerchief and apron and headcloth. Granny, whose old face was like those of proud bronze statues Harriet had seen: high, carven nose flaring strongly at the nostrils; eyes deep-socketed; cheek planes flat; mouth long and cleanly cut, flexible for speech and laughter, firm for closure. Granny, fit child of Moses.

The rest of the day sped like a strange dream. Dreamlike, surely, that Harriet Freeman, of Minneapolis, should belong in this sleepy cabin with its fireplace of clay and sticks. Strange that her only kindred should be an old woman who looked like an Ethiopian princess and spoke a language bewildering to the ear.

Lily, the drift, showed Harriet the immediate surroundings. Grinning and darting ahead and capering back, she led the way down through the thicket where the mockingbirds sang, parting curtains of gray moss as she went. She darted out upon a sandy beach and the fiddler crabs scuttled into their holes with an elfin patter, lugging their grotesque 'fiddles.' She jabbed a small finger toward a gray shack standing on stilts above the water. 'Oyster-shuckin' fact'ry!' she announced, finding her voice again.

Far away a whistle shrilled. 'Da's where at ey cans s'rimps,' she said hoarsely.

Sea smells; lush swamp smells; perfume of unseen flowers. Harriet came up on her toes and spread her arms wide and sent her voice spiraling upward exultantly, as they turned back toward the cabin.

The deep dust of the back yard had been patterned like an engraved tablet by the feet of Granny's motley crew of hens. The hens pecked busily around the door, and a hound, Caesar, thumped his tail to greet them, and a cat, Snowball, stretched herself in the long rays of the sun. With her small stomach importantly thrust out, the drift picked up an armload of brush and deposited it beside the kitchen fireplace.

Granny was stooping above a kettle that swung over the fire. She smiled at Harriet.

'Hopes y'all hungry!' she said, uncovering an iron spider that steamed amid the embers. 'Granny done fry y'all a chicken, honey chile.'

'I never was so hungry in my life,' Harriet said with conviction. 'What's the other good smell, Granny?'

'Hoecake, honey? Sho' y'all knows hoecake? Or does you maybe mean de sweet 'taters?'

Granny served the supper on the crowded kitchen table. She took from her trunk a yellowed linen cloth and spread it with careful hands. The dishes she placed on the clean, darned fabric were cracked and miscellaneous. One plate was old blue, one was cheap pink, the rest were ten-cent-store white. But the flavors were such as famous chefs might lick their lips over.

After they had eaten, Harriet wiped the dishes, and they all sat on the porch a while, none of them saying much. Even Mr. Trindle's conversation petered out, and he politely covered one yawn after another until Granny, gently thudding in the rocker, rebuked herself.

'Y'all tired out. I ain' got no sense, neither no manners, tonight. Reckon I cain' study nothin' but my li'l gran'' — she patted Harriet's shoulder — 'But y'all come a far piece an' you needs yo' rest.'

With ill-concealed eagerness they went in. Mrs. Trindle's eyes gleamed as she contemplated the bed. What can be more beautiful to the traveler than smooth, white pillows and a crisp, white sheet hem competently turned over the covers?

Granny folded back the pieced coverlet. It was far too warm for a quilt.

'Harrie, do look!' Mrs. Trindle exclaimed through a yawn. 'Wouldn't they be wild over that quilt in Minneapolis? And the bedstead, too. Hand-made. And — yes,

GRANNY

sir! cords instead of springs. — Mrs. Freeman, how long have you had it?'

Granny chuckled deeply. 'Honey, don' go askin' me how long. My fader fetch me here jest after Marse Lincum turnt us loose. An' here I been ever since, an' dat dere bed wid me. An' I pray de Lawd E lemme stay here twell E call me home to Heaven.'

'If you were up North, they'd be pestering you to sell that bed,' Mrs. Trindle said practically, caressing the well-rubbed wood.

'Law, honey, don' nobody hanker after ol' truck like dat when ey kin get shiny gol' ones,' Granny protested.

'But, Granny, haven't you read how crazy people are for old furniture and things? In the cities up North?' Harriet asked shyly.

Granny laughed a rich laugh that shook her tall body and sent her earrings glinting in the lamplight. 'Y'all funnin' yo' ol' granny?'

'Funning you? Why, no, Granny. Surely you've read about it yourself.'

'Hab mussy!' Granny said amusedly. 'I cain' read, honey chile.'

Harriet's heart plunged. It seemed — outlandish — to have a grandmother who couldn't read. Harriet Freeman, member of the Honor Society at Centennial High. Harriet Freeman, whose father had been a university graduate and whose mother had been valedictorian in normal school.

Without hope she murmured, 'You mean — your eyes aren't strong enough, Granny?'

Granny shook her head comfortably. 'Ain' never read an' write, honey chile.'

Harriet lay on her pallet on the floor a long time that night, staring through the darkness that lay like a thick, hot blanket over her, and thinking how strangely everything had turned out: Landers School and Granny's

25

'homestead' and Granny. No, not Granny herself. She was as stately and beautiful as an old woman could be. Even her folded coif was stately, not unlike an Egyptian headdress, when one got used to it.

But — Granny's illiteracy! Harriet could not subdue a sick shame at thought of it.

To live with it was unthinkable. She would be as good as she possibly could, during the few days before the Trindles must start homeward. Then she would go back with them and make better use of her opportunities than she had ever done. She would really work with all her might at her dear music, so that some day she could compose something that should hold the magic sounds of sea and wind and birds, and even of the frogs she could hear through the dark, drowsily; the magic sounds and the enchantment that held them all.

Once a week, regularly, she would write to Granny. She quivered at the thought that R. Corwin would have to read those letters to Granny. She hoped she need not meet R. Corwin.

The frogs piped and the chorus of the crickets rose and fell through the sultry darkness, and Harriet was asleep.

III

R. Corwin

Harriet woke reluctantly when Lily, all dressed, stepped carefully over her, carrying her own folded bedding to the rail of the back porch to air.

The atmosphere was still as steamy as a Turkish bath, but Harriet felt her hunger stirring when she sniffed the rich smells of coffee and baking breadstuff. Granny was bending over the hearth again, shifting a hot sheet of metal where the flat corncake was baking.

While the Trindles were bestirring themselves, Granny killed and dressed a chicken and set it frying in a three-legged iron spider in the fireplace. In another pot green pods bubbled, with a ham bone to flavor them.

'You mean y'all ain' know *okra?*' Granny answered her query in amazement. 'Honey chile, wha' kine of vittles does you-all eat up No'th?'

The church house, Granny told them at breakfast, was a far ways and the weather looked juberous — so heavily sultry. 'But Preacher Smith gwine fetch you,' she added with a pleased smile. 'So us better get ready tereckly.'

Five people preparing for church in two small rooms made a gentle bedlam: dressing behind doors, stumbling

over each other in unconventional attire, continually need-
ing something that had been left behind someone else's
door.

Betweenwhiles Lily fed the hens and the young 'critter,'
work ox, Nicodemus, and threw scraps to Caesar and set a
saucer of milk for Snowball. And Granny stirred and tasted
and seasoned savory dinner dishes and packed a huge
basket and attended to the milk — 'Neighbor chile done
milk fuh me.'

Lily had had her bath on Saturday, she informed Harriet. Today she needed only a washing and the rebraiding
of her small pigtails. Harriet counted twenty of them,
each rising straight from the center of its own little patch,
each patch bordered by an even brown pathway. Granny
unwrapped one braid at a time and combed it, while
Lily writhed and rolled her eyes to make sure that Harriet
appreciated her anguish; then Granny rebraided and re-
wrapped it. Clean long stockings were pulled on Lily's
thin legs and held up with firm twists of cloth; a patched
and skimpy dress, beautifully ironed, was dropped over
the pigtails. She was finished.

Thereupon she flew around importantly, helping others.
The pump was in the back yard, and she rode the squawk-
ing handle again and again, and lugged in pails of water.
Dumbly she pointed out the two square inches of mirror
on the kitchen shelf, and Granny's clean fragment of
comb. Open-mouthed she watched Harriet use her own
comb and toothbrush and powder puff and rouge.

'Preacher Smith,' tall and portly and golden brown, was
tapping at the door during the last bustling hurry, and
he bowed them out to the rusty automobile that chugged
and shivered in the road. The two ministers and Lily
crowded into the front seat, and Granny and Mrs. Trindle
and Harriet wedged themselves into the back, smoothing
themselves down as compactly as possible, so that the

crowding and the moist heat together should not quite wreck the freshness of Sunday clothes. Even the moving car gave no illusion of coolness today.

'Approximately what would you opine to be the dimensions of this enchanting little isle?' Mr. Trindle inquired.

It became immediately apparent that 'Preacher Smith' also enjoyed conversing. He did not slacken till they drew up before the church, and by that time the guests found themselves as fully informed as if their noses had been buried in a guidebook.

The island, said the minister, was fifteen miles long and four wide, and had a population of some thousand Negroes and fifty white people. In early days the famous Sea Island cotton had been grown here, and made the plantation owners rich. Boll weevil and the fall in the price of cotton had ended its great value as a crop.

At the close of the Civil War the land had been sold to the freed slaves at a nominal price — about a dollar an acre — in small farm tracts. In many cases their descendants still held the same ground, growing garden truck, cane, a little cotton, a little rice. But many of them had fallen behind with their taxes, and much of the land had been sold from under them by Northerners who used it for winter homes and hunting preserves. Of late it had also been in demand for truck gardening.

'If our people could only hang onto their land,' Mr. Smith concluded. 'They could have a mighty nice life here, mighty nice. Fish and s'rimps and oysters for the catchin', and rabbits and partridges ——'

He sent his old car bucking and shivering through the white coral dust. Harriet was thankful that they were late. At the church house, set far from any other building in the misty, gray wood, she found swarms of new faces turned toward them. She was glad that they must press through the waiting groups and take their seats without pausing to talk. With smiling, gold-toothed bows right and left, 'Preacher Smith' led the visiting minister up to the platform and opened the service.

Jericho Church had no hymnals, no organ, no piano, but it had music that swept its oblong, whitewashed box like an ocean tide of splendid sound. Harriet had heard spirituals all her life, but never anything quite like the great ebb and flow of these. 'Great Day, the righteous marchin', God gwine build up Zion's wall!' — 'Oh, Lawd, come by here!' — 'Let your light shine over!'

Feet beat time, bodies swayed, the close, hot church throbbed with the rhythm like a pulsing heart.

The pastor introduced Mr. Trindle, who read the Scripture, looking smaller, darker, larger-eyed than ever in the dimness of the church. The pastor preached, and the whole congregation nodded and sighed and moaned and called, 'Amen!' and 'Hear him, Lawd!' The pastor called for prayers, and Harriet felt her great-grandmother stir at her side and gather herself together and stand.

Through half-open eyes Harriet could see the big dark hands clenched on the bench-back. Granny's husky voice broke on the murmurous congregation. 'Oh, dear King Jesus,' she prayed, 'we done come yere to praise Yo' Name!'

'Praise de Lawd!' someone echoed.

'When de way seem dark, Lawd Jesus, an' it look like us all alone in dis big worl', he'p us to remember dat You ain' never fuhgit us. Forgive us our foolishment, King Jesus!'

'Do, Lawd, do!' the voices chimed in, and the church pulsed again with the patting of feet.

Fans fluttered more and more rapidly as the service went on; and at its close people detached their shoulders cautiously, with a ripping sound, from the seat-backs, and went outdoors, where it was scarcely cooler.

Dinner was served under the great trees, on planks set up for tables. Busy, jolly women heated kettles and pails of food on a stove in the detached kitchen — though Harriet wondered how anything could possibly have got cool in this atmosphere. The congregation stood before the well-filled board and sniffed the savory steam that rose from a score of dishes, until Mr. Trindle had asked the blessing long and sonorously. Then hearty voices and high laughter were set free in a great burst of sound, and the busy, jolly women poured hot coffee and loquaciously urged food on the assembled people.

'Mo' collard greens, Rev'end? Mo' s'rimp?'

'Lawzy, Mis' Freeman, y'all ain' eat *nothin'*. Reckon you just too proud of yo' gran'.'

'Sis' Brown! Got some mo' Hoppin' John in that dish?'

The fat, jolly women waddled gaily to and fro with their savory dishes, their brown faces dimpling like pricked bread loaves. The thin jolly women skittered to and fro, quick as bantam hens, and shrieked with good-natured laughter. The men shouted and slapped their knees and guffawed. And everyone ate as fast as possible. To Harriet it seemed like a big, rollicking picnic; and she thought it was good to have it all tied to the little whitewashed church.

There were girls among the diners, but not many. They edged away from Harriet and averted their eyes when she looked at them. There were boys, in noisy clusters.

One boy Harriet particularly noticed. A grizzled hound with a tattered ear got up from the ground when this boy came out of church, and pressed an adoring nose into his hand. Lily had run to him, too, and he had swung her up on his broad shoulder as if he were used to teasing and petting her. He ate across the table from Harriet and some distance down, and she looked at him whenever she had a chance.

He was tall and slim, with a good, strong flash of white teeth in the warm brown of his face. His head was well shaped, and the tight rolls of curly hair that covered it made Harriet think of the curls of the old Greeks. His neck was a trifle too long, though it could stand extra length, it was so strong and round. He wasn't exactly handsome, but his eyes were: straight-looking, brown eyes with gleams of amber, almost hidden by thick lashes when he laughed. Harriet had observed that people with eyes like that didn't need much else to make folks enjoy looking at them. As to his clothes, his trousers had been worn shiny and his clean shirt was patched; but his orange necktie was knotted with firmness and a certain style.

Harriet cleared her throat two or three times before she succeeded in asking Lily: 'Who is the boy down the table? The one with the orange necktie?'

Lily had been eating with amazing speed and capacity. Now her well-picked drumstick shot out in the boy's direction. 'Who? Him?' she asked, her mouth full of chicken.

Harriet blushed. She looked down at her plate and pretended to be greatly interested in the collard greens there. 'Hush!' she whispered, and glanced furtively at the boy. He had heard Lily. He was grinning at her, a question in his glance.

'Dat-dah one?' Lily persisted.

'M-hm,' Harriet assented in a strangled voice. 'But, Lily, *don't point*. For goodness sake don't let him know we're looking at him.'

'Why, dat Richie,' Lily announced in a penetrating whisper, rolling her eyes cautiously toward the subject of discussion. 'E too nice, dat boy. E de bes' boy dey is.'

Harriet ate rice and shrimps as if there were nowhere in the world a tall, brown boy with laughing eyes and an orange necktie. She simmered with embarrassment.

RICHIE

She simmered with heat, too. The air was heavy and still, the trees motionless, the curtains of moss motionless.

'Isn't it — sort of breathless weather?' she asked Mr. Trindle, who stood at her other side.

The Reverend Mr. Smith leaned across the narrow table and answered, and his voice was anxious. 'It's portent-i-ous weather. My radio says this mo'nin' that the big sto'm's headed toward Florida, but I'm thinkin' we might get hurricane winds here.'

('Radio!' thought Harriet, 'how out of key with this sleepy island, this far Jericho Church!')

Mr. Smith was rapping the board with his knife-handle. 'I don' know but we-all better put out fo' home as soon as we are through eatin', brothers and sisters,' he announced in the hush that followed his gavel. 'Look a pow'ful lot like sto'm.'

The confusion of laughter and clattering dishes and talk gradually swelled again, but Harriet noticed that eating was quickened, and that people began to melt away, walking, or jogging through the woods in mule-drawn wagons or carts.

'Lily and I would just as soon walk,' Harriet suggested to Mr. Smith, 'and then there would be room for some other grown people. — I'd love to walk,' she added hastily, 'if Lily knows the way.' Mr. Smith looked dubious, but Harriet persisted; she wanted to see as much as possible of the island before she went back to Minneapolis.

'Sho' I knows de way,' Lily said indulgently.

'Thank you kindly,' Mr. Smith agreed. 'I'll likely meet you befo' you arrive and fetch you the rest of the distance.'

Because it was so hot, big girl and little one walked slowly. Lily strutted with pride and kicked up spurts of fine white dust with her clumsy little shoes. Harriet lifted her hat to let the air reach her damp forehead. A heavy silence blanketed the island; even the mocking-birds gave only an occasional fretful flute from the thickets.

'Y'all ever tas'e wil' grapes?' the child asked. 'I knows whah at dey's some big ol' vines.'

She darted from the road into a thicket where thick-bodied vines climbed high in the trees. 'Dasn't shin up in my Sunday clo'es,' Lily said wistfully, eyeing the clusters of shiny fruits overhead.

Harriet ran and leaped in air, swinging up a long arm. She clutched a cluster and handed it to Lily; got another for herself. The fruit was the more piquant because it had so little pulp and so much seed. Again and again Harriet leaped and brought down treasure.

A long pennant of moss brushed her cheeks as she stood eating, and she looked around her: everywhere the moss was swinging and the branches were waving.

'Reckon us better git goin'!' Lily said uneasily, and led the way through the copse.

Harriet went leaping along beside her. Heavy vines swung in her face. Long, thin vines caught at her ankles and twisted round her legs, pricking and tearing.

'I — didn't — know — these woods were — so deep!' she gasped.

Lily stopped stockstill. 'Dey — dey ain'!' she faltered. 'Reckon us done gwine de wrong way.'

Without discussion they wheeled in another direction. Still the woods stretched on. Harriet lifted her eyes apprehensively to the uneasy branches, for a sudden twilight fell, as if the sun had set or sea birds flown across the sky.

A new sound struck through the rush of wind and the creak of branches: a great roar of sound — boom — boom — boom! The woods thinned ahead of them and they dashed out upon a little ridge.

Lily burst into a wail. The ridge overlooked, not the

road nor someone's cane or cotton patch, but long lines of angry, steel-gray waves that came thundering in on the rush-grown beach.

'I don' know whah us at!' Lily sobbed.

The rising wind wrapped their skirts around their legs, turned Lily's over her head like an inverted umbrella, drove the salt spray into their faces. And then, as if the sky had broken, the rain poured down and sent them staggering back under the trees.

Lily cowered against Harriet, shaking with fright, and for a moment Harriet, too, gave way to panic. This was unlike anything she had ever known. Lost, it seemed, in a tropic storm!

She shook herself together. Lost on an island fifteen miles by four? Nonsense! They must have been running lengthwise of this narrow strip of woodland. If they struck a course at right angles to the beach, surely they would soon come out into the open.

An explosive report followed by a screech and swish sent them leaping. That sound could be nothing but the fall of a mighty tree limb, and a warning that the woods were no safe refuge. They pushed onward.

Wild screams of the wind lashing the trees, crack of branches, rush of rain, roar of driven bay waters! Harriet plowed on, Lily's cold, wet paw in hers. The grasp of the wind, suddenly seizing them and carrying them on across stubbly ground, told her that they had come out into a field, at last. She put her mouth to Lily's ear: 'Which way now?'

Lily, eyes screwed tight, shook her head and sobbed. The wind pushed them on until their lungs labored for breath. The rain drove through their clothes. Harriet braced her feet and tried to stand. She had never dreamed of such noise and fury. The whole world was one screech and bellow, one mad, buffeting, tearing clamor.

'Lie down!' she told Lily. 'Lie down till we can get our breath.'

A strong hand closed on her shoulder. She twisted around and looked up into the face of the boy Richie. The old hound cowered against him, head and tail tucked low.

'Oh, Richie!' Lily hiccoughed, burying her face against him. 'Oh — Richie!'

Tacking this way and that, Richie guided them across the stubble field, through a cane patch combed flat by wind and rain, in at a door that the wind almost snatched from its hinges.

'Praise de Lawd!' cried Granny. 'Mistah Trindle! Preacher Smith! Dey's here! De chillen here!'

For it was Granny's own cabin they had reached. Granny and Mrs. Trindle, gray-faced with fear, drew them into shelter, and Mr. Trindle and Mr. Smith turned back with obvious relief from the front door.

'Dey gwine fuh hunt y'all,' Granny explained, feeling Harriet and Lily with shaking hands. 'Go in behint de do' an' git you on some dry clo'es. Richie, reckon y'all do efn you wrap a coat roun' you? — Oh, praise de Lawd! I so purely scairt, honey chile!'

The seven people huddled round the fire as best they might, the girls and Richie shivering in spite of themselves. The storm was a monster, wrenching the trees, tearing the shakes from the roof, pulling at the doors, driving a spray of rain in at every crack. Above its wail and shout Harriet heard all at once the cackle of hens; and looking through the holes in the walls she dimly saw the hen-house turning somersaults across the yard; skittering along, bounding in the air, crashing against the fence.

The cabin was shadowy, with its windows shuttered. Granny lighted a lamp, muttering little prayers as she did so. The feeble flame flickered cheerlessly. The rag rugs rippled in the wind that blew through the broken floor, and lay in little drifts against the walls. Mr. Smith knelt by the bed and prayed aloud, and Mr. Trindle stood and added to his petition. Granny raised a spiritual and they all joined, though they could hardly hear their own voices. There was comfort in singing, 'Oh, Lord, come by here!' even to the accompanying screech of wind down the chimney, the battering of rain, the pelting of oranges on the roof; comfort, though the frail shack groaned and swayed around them.

Wind and rain lulled at last, and Granny opened a shutter and peered out. She fumbled it shut again, and when she turned, Harriet saw tears coursing down her face.

'Po' ol' fig tree!' Granny said huskily. 'Done went down dis time. Weathered lots of heavier sto'ms, but now it done fo'.'

Mr. Smith was buttoning his coat. 'Better go now, in this interval,' he said, and shook hands and departed.

The others grouped themselves round the door, which Richie held ajar, and listened till a series of muffled explosions told them the reverend car was still able to work.

Lily had been holding tight to Richie's sleeve, and when they turned back she demanded irrelevantly, 'Richie, how-come y'all fin' me 'n' Hayet?'

A deep flush reddened the smooth brown of Richie's face. He grinned, and the warm amber in his eyes glinted sidewise at Harriet through his furry black lashes.

'We-ell — reckon ol' Jess trail' you,' he improvised, twisting the old hound's ear gently. 'Couldn' make 'm quit, nohow. So I went along to see if she'd got track of a rabbit.'

Granny chuckled.

'I ain' like the look of the sky,' Richie said frankly, 'neither the feel of the air. And when Lily turned off through the woods, I reckoned Miss Harriet might get scared in the storm. It wasn' much outen my way.'

'Oh, do you live near?' Harriet asked. She wanted to say something casual: it was so silly to feel embarrassed before an ordinary island boy.

'Sho' nuff!' Lily answered promptly, nestling against him. 'E live nex' do'.'

'Why, honey chile, y'all knows Richie,' Granny said in her comfortable way. 'E done write letters to you-all.'

Harriet looked at him blankly and shook her head. 'You must be thinking of someone else,' she protested, her voice thin against the storm.

Richie pulled his close-cropped curls with his free hand and made a quaint, foot-scraping bow. 'No'm, Granny ain', Miss Harriet. Ain' you recognize me? I'm R. Corwin.'

IV

YOUNG GRANNY

R. CORWIN! It astonished Harriet to have her vague picture of a middle-aged woman fall suddenly to pieces and reshape itself into this boy with his slim length and broad shoulders and laughing eyes. She felt queer to think he knew so much about Granny and her, but she couldn't feel vexed with him.

And he looked definitely pleased with her. They stood staring at each other until Granny said: 'Richie, dis quiet spell cain' las'. Maybe y'all better —— '

'Sho' had!' he agreed, laughing at his own abstraction. 'Better go tell Mom we all safe.' He bowed himself out of the door and was gone.

'Oh —— ' Harriet exclaimed.

'E come back tereckly,' Granny responded with a chuckle. 'E de chile dat milk our cow.'

She bent stiffly to straighten the heaped-up rugs, and then busied herself rebuilding the kitchen fire, using no small fuel that could make dangerous sparks. When she lifted the lid of a kettle that stood simmering in the ashes, Harriet unconsciously moistened her lips and swallowed.

'Hoppin' John,' Lily announced, widening her eyes in

Shuttered Windows

anticipation and patting her small stomach. 'Bet Richie
stay to supper dis night.'

It was an hour later that a fumbling knock heralded
Richie's return. Lily whirled the wooden button and
opened the door, clinging to it with both hands as the
wind caught at it, and slamming it to and buttoning it as
soon as Richie was inside. He bore a pail of foamy milk
and one of water.

'Kind of early,' he apologized, 'but the sto'm ——'

'Dat cow all right?' Granny asked anxiously.

'Fine as silk,' Richard assured her. 'Only e don' let me
get much milk. Scared, I reckon.'

'Ma li'l critter all right, too?' Lily asked, rummaging
in his coat pockets while he was washing his hands, as if
she were used to finding small gifts there.

Wiping his hands, Richie slanted his gay glance down
at her, 'That Nebuchadnezzar ain' turned a hair,' he said,
looking from her to the other room as if he wanted to go
in but didn't know how.

Lily thrust out her lower lip at him. 'Nicodemus!'

'Nebuchadnezzar!' Richie teased.

'Nicodemus!' Lily whimpered.

'*Nicodemus* ain' eat no grass. — Oh, have it yo' own
way. — Nicodemus.' He tousled her braids and went on in.

Mrs. Trindle was rocking, and Mr. Trindle was standing,
hands clasped behind his back, teetering from heel to toe
while he peered at the papers pasted on the wall. He was
an inveterate reader, and the only print in the cabin was
the wall-paper and the Bible on the three-legged stand.

From the kitchen where she was straining the milk,
Granny called, 'Set down an' res' yo'se'f, Richie!'

He let himself down onto one of the stools and blinked
rapidly at the scallops of newspaper that trimmed the
mantel.

Harriet liked shy boys. With them she dropped the

40

scornfully indifferent manner she had for the more aggressive ones.

'I never did really thank you for saving us from the storm,' she said, raising her voice above the noisily increasing blasts.

Richard jerked his foot and tilted his chin as if he were making a bow sitting down. 'The pleasure was all mine!' he shouted.

Involuntarily they both laughed at his informal formality.

'Show him some of those kodak pictures, Lily,' Harriet suggested.

Lily, sitting on the floor with a sheaf of snapshots in her scanty lap, edged over to Richard's knee and thrust a picture at him.

'The Lincoln Memorial,' Harriet explained, leaning toward it. 'I took five rolls on the way, and had them finished while we were in Charleston. Lincoln Memorial came out pretty well, didn't it? It's — well, it's so beautiful it makes me feel awfully queer. I never felt that way about a building before, though the Empire State in New York — May I have the pictures a minute, Lily?' She shuffled through them and showed him the one she had taken from the tower.

'I seen Savannah oncet,' Richard said, looking respectfully from the picture to Harriet. 'Savannah's right pretty, but it ain' got nothin' like thisyere.'

The wind had risen high again, and Richard hitched his stool closer so that he could hear and be heard. Mrs. Trindle tied an apron over her chubby brown voile and joined Granny in the kitchen. Mr. Trindle made his way placidly across one wall, tipping up his head to read through the bifocals; when the wind rushed away for a moment they could hear his deep hum and Mrs. Trindle's cluck and Granny's husky murmur. Richie's voice, or

Harriet's, would blare out into the unexpected stillness.
Then the wind would be back again and the rain pounding,
and the two would raise their voices a notch higher, talking
as if to someone in the next house.

Lily stood first on one bare foot and then on the other,
behind the young people. Her mouth was open with
interest and wonder and her big eyes rolled toward
Harriet as she spoke, toward Richie as he answered, back
to Harriet, while she took them across the fifteen hundred
miles from Minneapolis, with the pictures for illustration.

'I ought to have a megaphone, and then I'd feel like a
sightseeing bus sure enough,' Harriet said, sitting back
and laughing weakly when she had reached Charleston
and her last snapshot.

'Y'all got any pictures from yo' home town?' roared
Richard.

'Oh, yes. I brought my memory book to show Granny.'
— Harriet prodded her suitcase from under the bed and
lifted a bulky scrapbook from it. 'This is Mr. and Mrs.
Trindle's house, where I live' — Richard stared hard at
the comfortable verandaed house — 'and here's our
school' — he sucked in his breath — 'and here's the
basketball team I play on. And Glee Club ——'

'*White* chillen?'

'We don't have separate schools. Separate places on
the street-cars and trains, either. There aren't so very
many colored people in Minneapolis. Goodness, I never
did see these — these Jim Crow compartments until I
came South. They make me feel like some kind of animal.'

Richie looked at her gravely. 'Minneapolis must be
like heaven,' he said.

Harriet laughed, shaking her head in vigorous dissent.
'Jiminy, no! We get snubbed plenty. — They are fair to
us in school, though. I played for the Glee Club, and all
the singers were white girls and boys. If you make good

you get the credit.' She tilted her stool sidewise to see what was on the page he was inspecting. 'Oh — those are our crowd: the kids I went round with. Iva and Helen' — she pointed to one after the other — 'are my best friends; and there's John and Dave and Jimmie.'

'Look mighty grand,' Richard said disconsolately. 'Dressed as nice as white folks.' He held the book closer, studying the boys' faces, their smart clothes. He glanced with polite interest at the girls, but returned to the page of boys.

'Which of theseyere —— ?' he asked constrainedly.

Harriet laughed. 'Which do I play around with? Well, mostly with this one: Jimmie. His dad's a doctor. Jimmie's going to be one, too, if he ever gets around to it.'

'Y'all spilin' yo' eyesight, chillen!' Granny shouted at them. 'Y'all better light de odder lamp.'

Richard, his face drooping, sprang to get the small lamp and light it with one of the twisted paper spills that waited on the mantel. He set the lamp on the three-legged stand beside the Bible and they drew their stools closer to its feeble yellow arc.

'You haven't told about your school,' Harriet remembered, thinking how strange memory book and pictures and favors and programs looked in this dimness of shuttered windows.

Richard's teeth flashed more happily. 'I go to Booker, over on St. Catherine's Island. Row myself over ev'y morning. Booker's great. Ain' no such a big place as yo' school, but it's sho' nuff great.'

'What kind? High school? Boys' school?'

'All kinds. Somethin' like Hampton. You-all knows Hampton. Booker teach us how to farm our land good and grow good critters and make good houses. Teach us how to mend our carts and make harness and fix shoes. Teach the girls how to cook and keep house nice.'

43

'But doesn't it have — well, lessons like algebra and history and — and English?' Harriet floundered, trying to be polite and at the same time to find out what she wanted to know.

Richard's face puckered in a rueful smile. 'Reckon y'all think we don't get no English, sho' nuff. It does seem like the islands and the coast got a diff'ent kind of talk, and it's hard to change it. Yes, m'm, we studies books along with crops and carpenterin'. It's a grand school.'

He unfolded from the stool as he spoke, and took from Granny's hands the bright pie tins of food she was carrying. Looking to see that Mr. and Mrs. Trindle had been served, he offered a tin to Harriet, 'pulling his foot' as he did so. The other tin he held out to Lily, with exaggerated deference. She giggled and shook her head. 'Gots to he'p Granny,' she said.

When all were provided, Mr. Trindle's resonant voice asked the blessing, and they ate.

Hoppin' John proved to be a concoction of rice and peas. Seasoned with slivers of red chili and hot from the kettle, it was no mean dish. The usual hoecake came with it, nutty and crisp; and hot cocoa.

Harriet sat at ease, relishing her food, feeling cozy and secure with the wind and storm trying to get at them and failing. She watched Richie thoughtfully in the dim light, her brows puckered. His eating manners were not repellent, even though he did break many rules of etiquette, holding the whole piece of cornbread on his palm to butter it, and dipping it carefully into the cocoa.

'Lily chile,' Granny rebuked the drift during the course of the meal, 'ain' I tol' y'all to don' leave yo' spoon in yo' cup?'

Richard hastily took his own tin spoon from his own tin cup and glanced sheepishly at Harriet. 'Yo' Granny is the most mannersable woman!' he murmured.

She leaned nearer him so that she need not speak so
loudly, and said, 'I wonder why she should be!' She had
noticed herself that Granny had no uncouth ways: some
that were strange and old, of course, like taking snuff.
But even the snuff Granny managed neatly.

'Maybe y'all can get her to tell about her great-
grandpa,' Richard said, as if that would explain everything.

'Moses?'

He nodded, swallowing hoecake. 'Seems like Moses was
quality. 'Sides which, Granny's folks was house servants.
Mine was field hands. Made a differ'nce, that did. —
Moses' white folks was dog-mean in they hearts, but
they was mannersable, and they learnt their Negroes nice
ways, and sense, too. Yo' Granny ain' even study signs
like most island folks — good-luck things and bad-luck
things. My land, she don't care if you put yo' hat on the
bed, even!'

Harriet glanced abstractedly at the bed and her hat.
'And yet Granny can't read or write.' She spoke wonderingly, forgetting her shame. No one but Richie and Lily
could hear, even with her voice pitched high, for the rain
was roaring again and the wind furious after a brief lull.

'Folks say Black Moses could read and write some other
talk like nothin' ever seen hereabouts. Like enough it
ain' true.'

Harriet screwed thoughtful brows. Would there be
any chance to get these stories from her great-grandmother
before starting home? Not with Mr. Trindle talking on
and on, gently, steadily, with a roll of fine, well-chosen
words like a phonograph record. Mr. Trindle talked all the
time he wasn't reading.

He had been talking between bites, though no one
seemed to hear him. Now, when the noise outside suddenly
withdrew as if it were worn out, his voice emerged placidly

on the comparative stillness: '—— never experienced so violent a conflict of the elements.'

Granny bent an anxious gaze on him. 'I ain' exackly git de words,' she confessed.

'Mr. Trindle says he never saw such a storm,' Mrs. Trindle interpreted briskly. 'And I'm sure *I* didn't.'

Granny's eyes narrowed into a far look and she shook her head. 'Dis li'l wind an' rain ain' been nothin',' she said indulgently. 'Hit ain' been nothin'.' Her bowed shoulders quivered. 'De Gre't Sto'm, way back when my gran's was all bofe baby-chillen — dat was a sto'm, sho' nuff. One of 'm been dis chile's pa,' she recalled suddenly, with a fond look at Harriet. 'I could tell you-all big tales of dat sto'm, sho' nuff.'

Outside, the fury had remained a while away, leaving only a steady fall of rain on sodden ground. Inside, the fire crackled pleasantly. Plates and cups were empty.

'Oh, Granny,' Harriet begged, 'do tell us about it. We can wash up the dishes afterward.'

'Hit too old an' far off,' Granny dissented.

'Your personal reminiscences of the disaster would be of great interest to us all, Sister Freeman,' Mr. Trindle urged, tilting back his stool so that he could cross his knees.

Granny looked at him admiringly. 'Rev'end, you-all sho' got de gif' of tongues.'

'Granny, *please* tell us!' Harriet pleaded, hitching her stool over close to the old woman. Richard muttered, 'Excuse me!' and tiptoed to pile wood on the fire, for the storm had made the air clammy. Granny stroked Harriet's hair tenderly. Lily's head nudged jealously into her and she stroked it, also. Her eyes were on the flicker of flame.

'Hit de wuss sto'm ever I knowed,' she mused aloud. 'I mind it good. A young woman I was den — risin' thirty-fi' — ; an' pow'ful, else you wouldn' be here dis

day, honey chile. — Us done pick de cotton, me and yo'
gre-granddaddy, and ready fuh dig de sweet taters.
Hit come like de sto'm today, on'y se'm times wuss ——'

The firelight sent the shadows leaping across the
ceiling, shrinking down to the floor. It glittered on Mr.
Trindle's gold spectacle rims and on Mrs. Trindle's
brooch. It illumined Lily's wondering eyes and dropped
mouth, and Harriet's intently knitted brow as she sat
with elbows on knees and chin in hands, gazing into the
fire while she listened, or turning to look with wonder and
sympathy and admiration into the face of Granny, now
impassioned, now anguished. It shone on Richard, whose
eyes rested most of the time on Harriet; on her intense and
lovely face; on her long, strong, sensitive fingers; even
on her warm-colored, prettily made dress.

Granny told the story in vivid, simple words, as if she
were thinking aloud, and the little group of listeners were
so carried along by the narrative that they lost all sense
of the cabin, the time, and were with Lucy Mary Freeman
in 1893.

She had been living with her husband in a cabin on
this very site when the great storm came. With them
had lived their son and his wife — eighteen or nineteen
years old — and their two children, Harriet's father and
his baby sister.

The hurricane had come from the West Indies and
smitten them with unleashed fury. The sea had risen
twelve feet above the high-tide mark, covering much of
Gentlemen's Island and the other islands. The sea swept
up in a lashing fury of spray, and the skies opened and
let down blinding torrents of water, and the wind hurled
itself, shrieking, across the land.

— 'Us soon see hit ain' no common sto'm,' said Granny,
shaking her head in fearful recollection. —

Her son went out to try to save the critter and the

cow. Minutes passed. The girl wife staggered out to look for her husband. Granny's man rushed after her. None of them came back.

Granny had looked down at the little baby, sleeping peacefully, 'in dis se'fsame bed, min' you!' and at Harriet's father, clinging to her knees and whimpering with fear, and she saw that their lives depended on her.

— 'I had it from de Lawd!' she said solemnly. —

She knew the cabin must go; but in the yard were trees; and in the trees, she felt, was her only hope. There was not time to get to the Big House — No, it must be the trees.

The chinaberry was out of the question: shallow-rooted, it would be jerked loose in an hour. But there was a live-oak, huge, old, clinging deep and tenaciously.

The cabin was groaning like a living thing, rocking as if in torment. Granny snatched up the baby, bundled her in a quilt, tore a stout homespun sheet with a mighty wrench of teeth and hands, and bound the strips around the cocoon of quilt and baby.

— 'E li'l brack head like a li'l brack flower in de midst!' Granny crooned, and her eyes were wet with tears after forty years. —

She opened the door, the baby girl in her arms and the two-year-old boy catching at her skirts. They were in the midst of a howling fury. She held the baby to her breast so that its breath should not be snatched away. Even Tommy's crying was wrenched from him and he was gasping and voiceless.

Granny ran for the oak tree, but even amid the harrying of the wind she lost the feel of Tommy's hands on her skirt. She went back and picked him up from the ground and carried him under one arm and the baby under the other. She fought her way to the oak and cowered against its trunk for breath.

Young Granny

How could she climb it? Climbing a tree took more than legs, and both arms were filled. Could she leave one child while she bound the other in the branches? She dared not. Pine shakes from the roof, stones from the chimney, hurtled through the air. Between her powerful teeth she gripped the strong homespun of the baby's bindings, swung Tommy like a sack under one arm, and climbed into the twisting, writhing, trembling tree.

Up among the broad branches, she tied the baby securely with the homespun strip, as she had planned. She tore her stout petticoat into more strips and trussed Tommy to another branch. She wedged herself into a place between them and waited. — She waited. Drenched and shivering, she waited.

Always she watched for any sign of her husband, of her son, of his young wife. But with no hope. For a while she could make out the dim shape of the cabin; then it was not there. The chinaberry tree was not there.

Shrieking clamor of wind. Pouring rain. Beating flood. Nightfall: grayness grown black. — Daybreak: blackness grown gray.

— 'But, Granny, what did you do all the time? What did you *do?*'

'Ain' do nothin' but pray de good Lawd Jesus. Ain' nothin' else fuh do.' —

Probably a day and a night she clung there. Then, doubtless, something struck her on the head, stunning her. At any rate, she found herself hurtling along in the wildness of black water and lost consciousness again. In the morning she was picked up among the wreckage on the shore near Bosquet, and carried into a building there.

— 'Honey chile, hit dat Wash'ton Hall at Landers School! Dat God's trufe!' —

When she was taken back, frantic, to Gentlemen's Island as soon as relief boats could go, they found the old oak one of the few trees standing on the island. Among its branches hung two-year-old Tommy, without sense or feeling, and the baby girl, dead.

— 'But Daddy never told me.' 'E ain' mo'n se'm year old when dem whi' folks took 'm up No'th,' Granny explained. —

No building on the island was left standing; not even the Big House; not more than a half-dozen trees. Half the people were dead. Disease took added toll because of the unburied bodies. That is, they were buried close to shore, and the tides soon uncovered them.

— 'My folks, dey says, "Die by water, Lie by water."'—

The few mournful, half-naked survivors worked painfully, burning the marsh sedge that had buried their farm tracts and their unharvested sweet potatoes, building shelters from the wreckage of cabins and houses, from the wreckage of a ship that was thrown ashore by the tempest. The Red Cross, with Clara Barton working in person, brought food and clothing. Granny and Tommy were given two pecks of grits and two pounds of pork each week.

With Tommy to live for, Granny had worked like a man. Neighbors had helped her raise a new cabin — this cabin.

'An' I root aroun' an' I root aroun', an' what y'all think I finds, all bruck up amongst de trash? Disyeah bed and deseyeah stools. Dat why I hope de good Lawd lemme keep'm twell I dies.'

Richard cleared his throat respectfully. 'Ever I hear tell that the first wild beanies came up on Gentlemen's after the sto'm.'

'Beanies?' Harriet asked, stirring like one waking from a long dream.

'Some calls 'em Po' John 'n' Polly. Them wild bean plants that stan's higher'n your head. — From seeds the waves fetched from far-off lands,' he added, dreamy eyes on the fire.

Young Granny

Mr. Trindle drew a long breath and pulled his watch from his pocket. 'Ten o'clock!' he proclaimed in his full round voice.

Harriet got up and staggered to the door, her feet sound asleep and heavy as lead. She pulled open the door a crack. After the tumult and confusion of the evening's story it was a surprise to find the wind almost dead and the rain falling heavily, quietly.

V

'SHO' NUFF?'

ALL that night the wind blew fitfully and the rain fell, but the next day dawned as peacefully as if storms had never been.

Granny and Harriet threw all the shutters wide to sun and air, and spread the bedding over the porch rails to catch the sunshine. Drenched ground and drenched wood steamed as the day drew on.

Green oranges sprinkled the scanty wet grass in the front yard, the mud in the back. The big-lobed leaves of the uprooted fig tree had not yet begun to droop. Granny hobbled around it, shaking her head, as she thought of the little green thumbs of fruit that would never thrust out from it, never ripen to richness, again.

The hens, which had perched disconsolately in their broken coop, came clucking and singing for food. Caesar thumped his lank tail in the sun, and Snowball rubbed against their ankles with a silken hum of flattery. Nebuchadnezzar-Nicodemus bunted Lily exuberantly. Butterflies like living flame danced on the orange and brown marigolds.

As soon as the old live-oak had dried out a little, Harriet clambered up among its branches. She clenched her teeth,

holding the homespun strips that bound the soft bulk of
the baby. She gripped the limp wriggle of little Tommy
under her left arm until it ached. She dragged herself up
with her right arm. She spread her toes inside her oxfords.
— Here — here! this might be the right branch for binding
the baby girl. This for the little boy. And here she could
wedge herself ——

'Harrie, dear, do be careful of that good skirt!' Mrs.
Trindle cautioned from below. Harriet's fierce frown relaxed and she laughed and adjusted the skirt and placed
her feet more carefully, so as not to scar their smooth
leather. She had been, not Harriet but Granny — Lucy
Mary Freeman, barefoot, clothed in linsey.

She settled in the gnarled branches, among the polished
little leaves and the long streamers of silvery moss that
hung down like the silver trimmings on a Christmas tree.
The hurricane could be the theme of a symphony. Its
crash and moan and roar swept through her ——

Morning sped, and afternoon.

'Do you think you can adequately complete your visit
with your great-grandmother by the day after tomorrow,
Harriet?' Mr. Trindle asked.

Harriet soberly studied a rag rug. 'I feel as if it were
sort of running away. When I think of Granny, with that
baby and my father ——'

'My dear child, you must not cloud the issue with
irrelevant facts,' Mr. Trindle advised. 'Some undertak-
ings are unnecessarily onerous.' — Mrs. Trindle folded her
small mouth tight, and her nod agreed with him — 'Even
in the North, I grant you, we have our handicap. But
there is no soul on this green earth who has not a handicap.
Some have poverty. Some have the curse of great wealth.
Some have ill-health. Some, my dear Harriet, have the
greatest handicap of all, which is to have none — nothing
to build bone and sinew of the spirit. Now we have the

handicap of color in a white country. Some of us think
about it so much that it hides all other handicaps from our
minds, as a dime can hide the sun if held close enough to
the eye. Color is not the only disadvantage; it is by no
means the greatest one; but if you were to remain in the
South, Harriet, you would double it, at least.'

Mrs. Trindle slid into his pause-for-breath. 'Granny is
comfortable and contented, with Lily to love and to run
errands for her, and this Richard ——'

'There is one matter' — Mr. Trindle rolled the words
from his tongue slowly but without relish — 'that it may
be necessary to investigate. I chanced upon it yesterday
while following the course of a serial story around the
walls. It has considerably troubled me.' He was pushing
back behind the headboard of the bed as he spoke, and
Mrs. Trindle was following. 'It may have been attended
to long since,' he said doubtfully, laying a long forefinger
on a newspaper pasted in the corner.

Harriet sidled along the bed so that she could see. The
newspaper sheet held gray columns of fine print, and at the
point of Mr. Trindle's finger the name, 'Freeman.'

Harriet read, her brows knitted: 'Freeman, Lucy Mary:
Gentlemen's Island, twenty acres, improved.'

'What's it about, Papa?' Mrs. Trindle inquired.

The finger traveled to the top of the page and pointed
out the caption, 'Real Estate Sold for Delinquent Taxes.'

'Y'all fin' sumpn eyesightin'?' Granny asked politely
from the doorway.

Harriet gulped and blurted out her question: 'Granny,
this says — Granny, did you know your place had been
sold for taxes?'

She gazed at Granny desperately, but the old woman
did not look surprised or frightened: only sad. She
smoothed down her gingham apron and stared across the
bed at the newspaper as if she could read it.

'So dat's whah e went to. Richie, fetch me de paper an' read 'm off to me, and I fold'm away on a shelf. Reckon I done pas'e 'm on by mistake sometime.'

'But, Granny ——'

'At what time was this occurrence, Mrs. Freeman, if I might be so bold as to inquire?'

'Long time ago,' Granny said vaguely.

'And have you heard no more about the matter? Has there been no attempt to — to remove you from your cabin?'

Granny's fingers shook as she straightened her head-cloth. 'No, suh, ain' nobody come near. Reckon de good Lawd gwine keep 'm off twell I's through wid dis earth.'

Harriet looked more closely at the paper. There was no date remaining. Rather blindly she stood staring while the others edged out into the room again. A small hand slid into hers.

'Hayet!' Lily whispered. 'Don' y'all crave to see de ocean? Spec' Richie want to take y'all, but I knows de way good as him.'

Harriet was glad to go, to get away where she could think, or maybe just feel. So she followed numbly as Lily capered on ahead. Burs rode her skirt hem, to claw viciously at her legs; thread-and-needle twined its tearing length around her ankles; cockspur worked in between oxfords and stockings; showers of water from the wet brush drenched stockings and draggled skirt. She gave them no heed.

And then Lily, grinning back at her, pressed through a tangle of vines, led up an unexpected bank of white sand and over a ridge, and presented the ocean.

'Ain' e *too* pretty?' cried the imp.

In long lines of jade the breakers swept in, topped by curling white foam as far as the eye could see. Endlessly they broke on the narrow strip of sand where lay no mark of man. On the landward side of the narrow strip the ridge was topped with a fringe of wild grain, slanted by yesterday's rain, its heads translucent in the low sun. There was no sound but the call of sea birds and the break of the waves.

Lily romped along the beach gathering shells into her skimpy skirt. Harriet stood looking as long as she could stand it, and then dropped on the sand and hid her face and cried.

It was beautiful here, but so different; so lonely. It was a world into which she did not fit. She could not stay here; she could not. She could not go to that school, with girls who spoke another language and had lived another life ——

But neither could she take Granny up North. Her small annuity would not care for the two of them there. And what would become of Lily if they were to attempt it? Yet if Granny's home was in danger ——

Lily tugged at her arm, got down on her knees, and pulled away her shielding hand and stared solemnly.

'Y'all — hongry?' She clasped her thin hands reminiscently over her thin stomach, as if that were the first cause for tears.

Harriet dabbed at her tears and sniffed. 'No. Are you?' she asked, her voice thick with tears.

Lily shook her head. 'Never no mo'. But, Lawzy, ain' I use' to be befo' Granny took me, down to S'vannah.' She rocked back on her heels, her skirt drawn tight around her bare ankles, and her face assumed a look of grave experience.

'Savannah? Did Granny get you in Savannah?'

'Preacher Smif, e fotch me. Caze I ain' belong to nobody. E fin' me eatin' vittles somebody frow to de dogs.' She giggled eerily.

Harriet shivered.

'I don' min',' Lily assured her. 'I ain' hongry no mo'. But I use' to cry an' cry. An' Granny use' to cry an' cry, too. — E glad to God, sence you-all done come to'm.'

Harriet scrambled to her feet and washed her swollen face in salt water that stung. That was the heart of the trouble. She meant everything to Granny.

Lily had stayed where she was, squatting on the sand, watching Harriet with shifting elfishness and pity. Now her head pivoted like a bird's, and she jumped up and ran toward the sand ridge.

Harriet wheeled, face and hands dripping, as the child swung possessively on Richard's arm. He was carrying a banjo slung over his shoulder, and the old dog Jess shambled at his heels.

'Done milk Granny's cow,' he explained. 'She reckon Lily taken you down along this way. She say y'all might like to see the sunset — it mighty pretty — and then come home to supper.'

'You play?' asked Harriet, trying to divert his eyes from her tears. 'Do play something, please.'

Richard stood at ease and thrummed his banjo. Thrummed old tunes that fitted the blue-washed cabin over the hill; queer tunes that Harriet had never heard. With the twang of the banjo came the soft low croon of words in a voice as rich as Jersey cream, or liquid and exultant as a meadow lark's song.

She listened, fascinated, until he paused and stretched an arm seaward. The sun was dropping, copper-red, into a low bank of cloud. They watched it fire the immensity of water before it, spreading a burnished golden pavement to their feet.

'Richard,' Harriet asked suddenly, 'what do you know about Granny's place being sold for taxes?'

'Reckon I know all about it. Way back in 1928, must 'a' been, when I was a young chile. Rich white man from up No'th — Yankee — he come projecking round and buy up a heap of thoseyere small farms that's back on their taxes.'

'Isn't there some law about owners having the first right to redeem their own property, though?'

Richard shrugged. 'They call it "double tax." Ain' many got cash-money to pay double tax.'

'Then why's Granny still in possession?'

'Seems like the rich folks up No'th got pow'ful po' all of a sudden, and thisyere white man ain' got money to build the grand house and stables and all.'

'But any time he wanted to, he could just put her out?'

'Reckon so. Lots of other folks in the same fix. Only I got my plans.' — Richard's glance kindled — 'If he hold off a few mo' years, till I done learn enough at Booker, I'm gwine teach my people how to farm so good they can pay taxes and git back the land.'

He stood tall and straight, unconsciously plucking chords on his banjo, and the last rays of the sun lighted him to copper.

'No place on this whole earth better to live, seem like, if on'y my people learn the good ways. Y'all cain' hardly know how po' most of 'em live, Harriet. Ain' had no chance. And that's what I want to do. I want to he'p 'em get a Rosenwald School. You-all knows Rosenwald Schools?'

Harriet nodded. The wealthy Mr. Rosenwald had established a fund from which half the cost of an adequate school building could be drawn by any community which would raise the other half itself.

'Then I want to be a Gov'ment teacher right here on Gentlemen's, and lead my people out into a grand new life on their own land.'

He halted in his eloquence and grinned at her self-consciously.

Harriet stared at him. She'd never seen a finer-looking boy. He looked like a leader.

'But, Richie,' she protested, 'you oughtn't to stay on this little tiny island all your life! Why — why, with your voice and — and everything, you could make a name for yourself up North, where you'd have some chance.'

Richard shook himself as if his own bright dream were fading like the golden pavement across the water. But Lily broke the momentary silence. She hurled herself on Richard, glaring over her shoulder at Harriet.

'E ain' gwine up No'th. E ain'! Efn you-all got to go off an' leave me'n Granny, you anyways ain' got no call to take Richie, too.'

Richard let go a sigh. 'Y'all — gwine back, sho' nuff?' he asked wearily.

VI

FIRST DAY OF SCHOOL

RICHARD's face had been the face of a leader looking toward the deliverance of his people. Now the joy had dropped from it as the sun had dropped from the sky, leaving him somber as the sea.

He glowed again when Harriet spoke.

'I'm not going away,' she said slowly. 'I'm going to stay and go to Landers School.'

Harriet had not known that she had decided until her own words told her so. The rest of that evening it seemed to her a good decision. Granny was so happy — 'I glad to God, honey chile. I glad to God' — and Richard and Lily; and the night was so mysteriously beautiful.

After supper they all sat out on the front porch. The two young people sat at the end and talked softly, so as not to disturb the older ones — or be themselves disturbed. Harriet told of the wonders of Minneapolis and St. Paul; wonders she had never recognized before: the chain of lakes, the high, wooded banks of the Mississippi, Minnehaha Falls, the marble loveliness of the Capitol, the art galleries ——

Richard had never ridden on street-car or bus or train;

never even in an elevator. He had never visited museum
or gallery. He sat clasping his knees and looking out
through the dusk where mocking-birds continued to call
now and then.

'It never seem real to me befo',' he said dreamily.
'Folks come a far piece — across the sea, even — and
visit Booker and tell us suchlike tales; but ever befo' it
seem like readin' in a book. When you tells it — a young
chile like we-all — then it do seem real.'

He touched the banjo strings with a gentle finger, and
the soft bite of the notes blended with the throaty voices
of Granny and Mr. Trindle, the dove moan of Mrs.
Trindle; with the contented munching of the cow, not
yet put in her shed; with the calls of birds and the swelling
and diminishing chorus of the crickets and the plaint of
frogs — even with the glimmer of fireflies. Harriet could
not untangle the elements that had bound her here: the
drowsy mystery of island days and nights, the majesty
and pride of Black Moses, and beautiful old Granny.

At the young people's end of the porch, talk ceased.
The banjo went whispering on; Richard hummed, and
Harriet joined in. For a little while the soft voices mur-
mured together. Richard sighed deeply, happily.

'Why'n't you-all sing befo'?' he demanded. 'Girl, y'all
sing good as me. Don't know but you sing better!'

Next morning, Harriet was less certain of her wisdom.
Mr. Trindle talked to her soberly, rolling his eyes up through
the upper section of his glasses because she was taller than
he — a fact which he would not, however, acknowledge.

'In the North, little girl, we enjoy comparative freedom
of motion and a sort of equality; while here — No, I am
fearful — if you will pardon the colloquial term, my dear
Harriet — I am fearful that you are biting off more than
you can chew.'

'I'll chew it!' Harriet vowed. 'I ought to be able to

stand anything for a year. And in that time I ought to find out what can be done about Granny and her place.'

'And your music?' Mr. Trindle persisted, blinking rapid eyes up at her.

'There'll be something I can practise on ——'

But it was a heavy gray day, inside and out, and it grew heavier and grayer as they took their farewell of Granny and Lily and Richard; as they steamed across the steely waters to Bosquet; as they motored along the black highway to Landers; as they made arrangements in the office for Harriet's tardy registration.

Today the campus was humming with life and activity, yet to Harriet it could scarcely have been more desolate. When, early that afternoon, she turned from the entrance gate and hurried stiffly to Washington Hall, the air pressed down on her unendurably. It was not soft, today; it was sticky. Beyond the draperies of gray moss Harriet could see the heavy gray of the bay. Crows swept across the gray sky, cawing hoarsely, and buzzards wheeled endlessly above her. The wind moaned through the trees and the bay moaned on the same dull, suffering pitch. Harriet tightened her lips as she went in at the door and climbed the steep stair.

For Mr. and Mrs. Trindle's car had vanished down the leaf-dark tunnel of road. They were on their way to Minneapolis. And she, Harriet Freeman, was a student enrolled in Landers School and shut away on this morsel of an island off one of the most remote corners of her country.

She frowned ferociously and snapped open a suitcase. She had pushed aside the blue calico curtain of her corner closet and was inspecting its half-spools nailed up for hooks, when she heard a mouse-sound at the door. She wheeled. A small, thin girl in a sack-like dress of bright red and pink, stood in the entrance, bent under the weight of an ancient straw bag and a matting suitcase.

'I MOSSIE CLAPP, F'M GREEN CO'NERS'

The small girl said breathlessly, 'Dee say downstairs I duh come to disyeah room.' She leaned out into the hall, rapidly counted doors, and nodded. 'Disyeah room.'

'I suppose we're room-mates,' Harriet said without expression. 'I was just about to hang my things in this closet. Does the other suit you just as well?'

The girl stared at Harriet with a dropped lip, and rolled big eyes from one corner to the other. 'Dee all bofe nice,' she sighed.

'We'd better introduce ourselves,' Harriet said unsmilingly, slipping a dress on one of the wire hangers she had brought and hanging it in her triangular cubbyhole. 'I'm Harriet Freeman, from Minneapolis, Minnesota.'

Another of those doubtful, blinking pauses. — 'I Mossie Clapp, f'm Green Co'ners. — Ain' nevah lef' mah home befo'.'

There was a frightened catch in her voice. Harriet glanced at her and away again. She was thin and obviously undersized for whatever age she might be. She was the imp Lily with a few years added.

Methodically Harriet hung her dresses: a brown-and-white checked taffeta; a striped organdy; a white Swiss with blue dots; a brown-flowered tan voile; a print; a wool skirt; sweaters; a semi-formal frock of brown chiffon, swirling over orange. As she picked up the chiffon, she saw that Mossie was shielding her own garments from sight, thrusting her body between them and Harriet, while she scrutinized each of Harriet's dresses with astonished eyes. Mossie's clothes did not take up half the hooks in her small triangle: two dresses — Harriet shuddered at the purple-and-yellow, the poisonous green — and nightgowns and underwear of sturdy, plain muslin.

Harriet took last from her suitcase the framed photographs of her father and mother. She looked for a place to set them. There was not even a dresser in this cubicle.

But there were nails in the board walls, and she contrived a way to hang the pictures near her bed, where she could see them early and late. Below them she thumbtacked an enlarged snapshot of the Trindle house. She had to frown more ferociously than ever when she was fastening up the pictures, and at the first clamor of the gong, she turned and ran out of the room. A glance at her wrist watch had told her it was the dinner bell.

She had never felt more alone than when she strode swiftly, head high, the length of the campus. Mossie was scurrying behind her, but Harriet felt too desolate to speak to anyone. Miss Francis, the principal, met her and placed her at a table with four other girls and Mossie, introducing them all.

The dining-room was gray from the clouds. Half the girls at her table were new, and the other half laughed and talked among themselves. Harriet was not hungry, and the food did not tempt her: okra and tomatoes and boiled potatoes and small portions of pork, with applesauce for dessert. She played with her serving, and made herself look around the room as if she were happy and quite at ease.

Of course there were attractive girls within her range of vision. She picked out a serious little dumpling with wide-set eyes and pretty manners; a willowy girl with a beautiful, tragic face; a large-framed, kindly one who made her think of a young edition of Granny; an arrogant one, modishly dressed, who regarded the scene coldly, under drooped lids. But at her own table there was no one who attracted her; and when they had finished eating and filed out, Harriet marched back across the campus alone, her head a half inch higher than before.

When she stepped in at the door of Washington, that blended odor wrapped itself around her, adding to her sense of suffocation: the musty smell and the sweetish damp smell; smells of wet vines and wet flowers, and ancient, worm-eaten wood, and the salt sea.

She rushed into her room and started to slam the door so that she might throw herself upon that narrow little bed and cry. — But she must not close the door: this was Mossie Clapp's room as well as hers; Mossie Clapp, a being out of another existence. — Harriet would have liked to crawl under the bed, but her two suitcases were there, since there was no other place for them. She sat down on the edge of the bed instead, and clenched her hands tightly together.

'Well, where under the sun did you hail from?'

A light, clear voice sounded from the door, and Harriet looked up, astonished, and into the ironic eyes of a girl who might have come from Minneapolis. Jauntily she stood there, a thin hand on each side of the door and feet nonchalantly crossed, and grinned at Harriet in delighted surprise.

'Minneapolis,' Harriet said feebly. 'Where did you?'

The other girl lifted her eyebrows and tossed her head in a comical gesture of uncertainty. 'Why — just here and there,' she replied, dropping boyishly on the other bed. 'Born in Jamaica. School in New York and Charleston. Mother was teaching French in Charleston, but she got a sort of bug to come down here — that was from Miss Bates, the music teacher here. She goes to Charleston one day a week. So we're trying this for a year.'

Harriet studied her with quickened interest. 'You mean you're going to go to school right *here?*' she asked, unconsciously patting the bed beside her.

'Sister, you don't know the half of it. Mah room's raght nex' do',' she said, impishly imitating the regional accent. 'What's your name, neighbor? We might as well get set without wasting any time. I can see we're going to save each other's lives, practically.'

Harriet told her, still regarding her with relieved amazement.

'And I'm Johnnie La Rocque, in case you want to know. It started out to be Jeanne, because we're part French; but I'm all for Johnnie. Fits me a lot better.'

Johnnie wore a boyish shirt, a well-tailored jacket suit, sport oxfords. The outfit suited her clever, singular face and straight, black, short-cut hair, just as the nickname did.

And her cool breeziness had swept away the heaviest of the clouds in the little room. Harriet clasped her knee and smiled at Johnnie, and told her how she had been missing Helen and Iva and Jimmie and the rest. She told her about Gentlemen's Island and Granny, and how, forty-three years ago, a young Granny in drenched linsey had been carried half drowned into this very hall. She even told her about Black Moses.

Johnnie laughed delightedly. 'My gosh, it sounds like a story-book! It isn't going to be so hard to get going here, after all. There's a teacher that's keen, too: white, but she can't help that. I mean, she's awfully young, for a teacher, and ought to be fun. And there are some swell-looking girls. — Oh, hello there!' she broke off cheerfully as Mossie Clapp sidled into the room. 'Come along, Harriet, and have a look at my diggings. Then we can see whether Mother's in her room.'

Both girls smiled at Mossie as they departed, but the smile shut her out instead of taking her in. Already, thrust together by the strangeness of their situation, the two were practically a closed corporation.

Mrs. La Rocque had a small suite at the end of the hall. Johnnie signaled her with a tuneful triple knock and escorted Harriet in. In spite of the severe wooden walls and the common furniture and the bleak wind that rattled the old-fashioned windows, the room seemed flooded with

sunshine and gaiety. Harriet couldn't see why, except that
the thin yellow curtains made a sunny glow and a chubby
copper teakettle jigged and chuckled on an electric plate
on the stove. The three women who looked up at the
girls' entrance added to the sense of coziness, one of them
curled up on a divan among yellow and orange cushions,
and all of them sipping tea from yellow pottery cups.

'Mother,' said Johnnie, when she had greeted the other
teachers, 'just lookit what I've found!' She pinched
Harriet's sleeve between thumb and finger and led her
forward triumphantly. 'This is Harriet Freeman. She's
from Minneapolis, so she comes pretty near being a darn-
yankee.'

Mrs. La Rocque grinned piquantly. Her high-curled
pompom of hair and the style of her dress were French
in their suggestion, and she looked the urbane gentle-
woman; yet her small, amber face with its enormous
dark eyes held a trace of Johnnie's *gaminerie*. 'I'm glad
you've come, Harriet,' she said. 'I told Johnnie she'd
find friends here. Miss Bates — Miss Anthony — may I
present Harriet Freeman?'

Harriet bowed. Miss Anthony, plump and sunny-colored and gay among the plump, sunny-colored gay cushions on the divan, showed two rollicking dimples and said
that Harriet had enrolled in her physics class.

'And Miss Bates teaches the music here and directs the
Glee Club and such matters,' Mrs. La Rocque observed.
'I don't know whether you're taking music or not, Harriet.'

Harriet murmured that she had not decided. She was
dubious about piano lessons at two dollars a month. Personally, this Miss Bates attracted her. There was an
obvious patch on Miss Bates's crisp gingham dress, as if
patches did not matter to her; but she carried herself
with distinction. She was so thin that her shoulder
blades showed plainly through her clothing, and the thin-

ness made her gentle, dark face even more sensitive-looking; yet with all the gentleness, her mouth was spirited and her eyes held fire.

'Won't you girls have some tea with us?' Mrs. La Rocque asked, pouring hot water from the chubby copper teakettle into the chubby pottery teapot.

Miss Bates had risen, glancing at her watch. 'A lesson,' she said, and sighed, with a significant, 'Ella Hooper!'

Harriet frowned determinedly. 'Thank you, Mrs. La Rocque,' she said, 'but I think I must go on. I wondered whether Miss Bates would let me walk over with her?'

She would ask to listen in on the lesson. How else was she going to find out what kind of teacher Miss Bates was — at two dollars a month? And it would be less embarrassing not to sign up for music at all than to sign and then cancel.

The lesson was as bad as Harriet could have dreamed. Ella Hooper folded herself on the piano bench in such a posture that Harriet wanted to sing her the song she had learned at camp:

> 'Are you a camel, or aren't you a camel?
> And say, do you have a hump?
> Do you sit at the table
> As straight as you're able,
> Or all in a lump,
>   lump,
>   lump,
>   lump,
>   lump?'

Yet Miss Bates did not correct the clumsy pose after a first patient suggestion. She did not correct the awkward position of Ella's hands. She let her go on, stumbling, faltering through the lesson without any form at all. Worse, she did not seem shocked or horrified or even bored. Her voice was gentle, patient; and if Ella approached a proper rendering of an exercise, the teacher clapped softly and said, 'Better, Ella; better!'

Harriet felt her face grow hot and her hands and feet large with embarrassment. When there came a pause, she rose hurriedly, mumbling a thank you, and that she would have to go and hoped Miss Bates would let her visit her again some day.

Miss Bates made as if to speak, and then nodded quietly, with a small smile folded into the sensitive mouth corners. 'Do visit me,' she said.

'Visit *her*, yes,' Harriet muttered fiercely to herself, as she was likely to be doing when she strode, head high and brows knitted. 'I do want to visit her, for I think she's lovely. But preserve me from listening to any more of her lessons. I can make some sort of excuse to Miss Francis about paying a dollar a month to use the piano in Jaynes Hall for practising; something about catching up because I'm behind. Goodness knows I am behind, away from a piano for weeks now.'

Miss Francis permitted Harriet the practice privilege, after the thoughtful scrutiny that always made Harriet stand straighter; and Harriet practised diligently, choosing times when there were few girls in Jaynes, or none at all.

The days went on with little change in the relations between Harriet and Johnnie and the rest of Landers.

'It's sure a lucky break that you and I have the same schedule,' Johnnie observed one day when they had got permits to walk beyond the school boundaries. 'When I have to cross that campus alone I feel as jumpy as if I were running the gauntlet. Or I feel like those dreams where you go to a party in the kind of knitted bedroom slippers your maiden aunt wears. You know: as if you were exposed to the public gaze and the public gaze was finding something awfully wrong with you.'

Harriet flicked her an incredulous glance. 'I thought it was just me that felt like that,' she said. 'No one would ever believe you gave one single hoot about anybody; not even the President of the United States.'

'That's hokum, though. A front you hide behind. You look, yourself, as if it would take the King of England to bow your proud head. That was what I noticed about you when first you came into classes: the way you stared down your nose at the world.'

Johnnie giggled impishly, but Harriet looked somewhat taken aback.

'*That's* a lovable manner!' she commented. 'Like Roseanne Gibbs.' Roseanne Gibbs was the modish and arrogant one she had noticed at her first Landers dinner.

Miss Senter was emerging from the office building as they passed it. 'Let's sort of loiter and see if she won't catch up with us,' Johnnie murmured. 'D'you know, there's another person that's lonesome, or I miss my guess. She's only here to fill a vacancy this semester. She's teaching Home Ec — the sewing part and dress design, and home decoration. Doesn't she look like a kid?'

The teacher did look as young as most of the high-school students: a slender, girlish type, with blonde curled hair.

She overtook them, and fell in step with them. 'Off for a walk?' she asked. 'So am I. Suppose we join forces?'

'That would be great!'

The three tramped down the black highway and into the woods, woods that plunged them at once into a deep strangeness. Single file they pressed ahead, weaving their way between great man-bodied vines and stepping high to avoid some of the burs and other prickly things that beset them. Mosquitoes rose in swarms, whining about their ears and stinging their ankles viciously. But there was a

70

recompensing beauty in the green dimness, the trees arching so high as to form a green sky.

At the edge of a clearing Miss Senter stopped abruptly. The other girls bumped into her and peered over her shoulders. Under the high trees lay scattered mounds of earth, vine-grown, weed-grown: little six-foot, seven-foot mounds.

'A — clock?' Harriet questioned in bewilderment. 'A — a teapot?'

'Good gosh!' shrieked Johnnie. 'There's a swell piece of old luster, or I'll eat my hat. It's broken, of course, but ——'

'I wouldn't disturb them,' Miss Senter said quickly.

Both girls gaped at her.

'It's a graveyard,' she explained.

There was a silence, in which Harriet felt herself gripped by something alien. Johnnie gulped, but she struck an attitude and saluted. 'Our dark ancestors!' she chirped.

Silently they picked their way between the graves, looking at their homely and pathetic decorations, their borders of colored glass or bright stones, their vases and teapots and plates and cups. Both fantastic and gruesome was that small cemetery deep in the woods, far from a settlement. It laid a pondering silence on them all as they tramped back to school.

'Why do you suppose they do that — put clocks and things on?' murmured Harriet, half angry.

'I've heard that they think it's a safeguard to decorate the grave with favorite possessions of the one who has died,' Miss Senter said diffidently.

'How do you mean, safeguard?'

'Why, so that the spirit won't come back and trouble the living.'

'Our people have a sweet lot of superstitions down here.'

'*Our* people!' Harriet protested. None of the three seemed to think of anything more to say.

As they reached the campus they could hear gay talk and laughter, a booming voice and snatches of song. A group of girls were studying on a bench under the sassafras tree, and laughing until they leaned helplessly against each other. Silence fell as Miss Senter and Harriet and Johnnie came in sight. The talk and laughter were clipped off as with sudden scissors, and every girl bent studiously above her book.

'Good afternoon, Willie Lou! Good afternoon, Ella! Good afternoon, all the rest of you whose names I don't know!' Miss Senter greeted them smilingly, but not until after Harriet had heard her draw a determined breath and had seen her square her shoulders.

Her small pleasantry fell into silence like a stone into deep water. Willie Lou lifted her smouldering eyes and swept the three with a hostile glance. 'Good evenin', Miss Senter,' she said coldly.

'Good evenin', Miss Senter,' murmured the other students.

When she was well past the group, the teacher shrugged unhappy shoulders. 'That Willie Lou's *bright*. But how she does hate and despise me. Why, do you suppose?' she asked, her gray eyes searching the other girls'. 'Of course none of them like me much, except maybe that cute little round Phyllodoxia, and Hannah Tomotley, and Pearlie Randall and her sister. — But with Willie Lou Bennett it's just plain hate.'

'She hates you for being white,' Johnnie answered matter-of-factly. 'Just exactly the way most white folks despise us for being colored.'

'But it doesn't make sense,' Miss Senter protested indignantly. 'Why did I come down here except that I like them?' She jerked her small head defiantly and smacked one fist into the other palm. 'And now I suppose they'll hate you for taking a walk with me.'

Harriet shrugged. 'What does it matter? They don't like us anyway. We two against the world.'

'One little, two little Injuns,' Johnnie chanted. 'Say, Harriet, why couldn't you and I room together? Let's ask Miss Francis this minute. Your Mossie isn't so bad, but you ought to listen to my Deena May. Jiminy, you can hear her laugh clear across the campus.'

'You can ask, but that's all the good it will do,' Miss Senter warned them with conviction.

She was right. Miss Francis looked at them across her neatly ordered old desk, her blue eyes a little amused, a little sorry and detached, as if no one's opinion could unduly sway her judgment.

'It would be a grave mistake,' she said. 'School isn't endurable if you don't establish yourself on a friendly footing with the majority.' She moved a book into precise alignment with the edge of her desk. 'And besides, I had hoped some of you girls who have enjoyed such rich opportunities—There are a dozen girls in Landers to-day who could give as much, in different ways, as the faculty — if they would.'

She patted the book decisively and looked up. The smile warmed her eyes. 'No. I'm sorry,' she said, 'but you must remain as you are.'

VII

Mostly Mossie

The girls made a polite exit from the principal's office, but they stormed mutinously along the walk to Washington Hall, and their rush up the stairs and along the squeaky corridor said more than words.

For once, Harriet slammed her door. It might be Mossie's room as much as hers, but even a dog wanted to be alone sometimes.

She was so sick of hostility; so sick of being surrounded by a hundred aliens. There was Phyllodoxia, the chubby one, of course, and Hannah, who looked like Granny, and the long-legged Randalls with their innocently wondering eyes. They might all be delightful if she knew them; but she didn't know them. And most of the girls had lived all their lives on the sea islands or on the coast, a background entirely different from hers. They neither liked nor understood her, and she neither liked nor understood them. Even Mossie stared at her with dropping jaw and scurried out of her way.

Harriet threw herself heavily on her bed. She would get a demerit at inspection for crumpling her spread, but she didn't care. She wadded her pillow and cried into it, letting loose all the tears that had been gathering since she had cried on the beach at Gentlemen's. She pounded the edge of her cot with her fists and kicked the foot of it with her shoes and then lay still for a long time, not thinking, only aching.

At last she sat up and began mechanically to smooth her hair. Of course Miss Francis meant well. In theory she was doubtless right. But couldn't she see that there was no common ground for Harriet and Mossie? for Johnnie and Deena May?

For the first time she noticed that the curtain of Mossie's closet bulged outward. She got up and lifted it. What she saw was funny, but it did not make her laugh.

Huddled in the cubbyhole with her dresses hanging around her, crouched Mossie. With swollen eyes she peered at Harriet between the skirt of a nightgown and that of her poisonous green Sunday dress. She sniffled forlornly and crept out. Trying not to look at each other, the girls sat on their beds, necessarily so close that their knees touched. Mossie sniffled again. Harriet blew her nose.

'I'm jest a-gwine die!' Mossie wailed suddenly. 'I wants to go home!'

'Well, why don't you?'

Mossie stared at her over a wad of handkerchief. 'I cain'. Mammy done pick cotton an' Pappy done pick cotton an' I done pick cotton; an' us all gone widout hoecake, even, fuh git de money. Cain' shame 'm all by gwine back.'

'Don't the other girls like you, either?' Harriet asked gruffly. 'They certainly don't have any use for me.'

'Dey scairt of you. You'n' yo' fine clo'es an' yo' gran' kin' — she nodded toward the photographs. 'An' me, I's scairt of *dem*.'

'But you certainly aren't afraid of me,' Harriet re-monstrated.

'I — I cain' make out yo' talk noway,' Mossie said feebly. 'Y'all duh talk so funny.'

'Oh, well. . . . We'll catch on to each other's lingo if we try hard enough.'

Harriet was thinking that Mossie's feeble drawl and hanging lip were like Stepin Fetchit's in the films. She had always thought the character an atrocious caricature. Well, there were as many different kinds of colored people as of white. Harriet emptied the last drops of water from the granite-ware pitcher and laved her hot face.

'You string along with Johnnie and me,' she said resignedly, when she came out of her fluffy towel.

After all, Mossie was more like a draggled little cat than anything else, and you couldn't leave a draggled little cat helpless.

'Wha' — wha' y'all say?' Mossie queried.

If only she would pin up that lower lip!

'Walk with Johnnie and me — sometimes,' Harriet said slowly and distinctly. 'And — I tell you what! Go with us to the picnic Saturday!'

'Thank y'all kinely,' Mossie murmured in a frightened voice.

At the same instant Harriet felt herself briskly kicked in the bend of the knees so that she almost sat down. She glanced over her shoulder: Johnnie had come in and was making a face at her, beckoning her with an imperative chin.

'It's all very well to go humanitarian,' Johnnie scolded, when they were out of earshot of everyone else, leaning over the balcony railing. 'But there's such a thing as carrying it too far. If you have to take up a protégée at all, why don't you adopt Phyllodoxia, or the baby-faced Randalls?'

Harriet tried to think of a convincing answer.

Johnnie tapped her foot impatiently. 'Well? — And

the picnic. I was looking forward to that picnic. But if your foundling is tagging us every minute, in that gingham dress that looks for all the world as if a blind and deaf and dumb person had cut it out with a can-opener in a dark room at midnight' — she warmed to her subject, her face losing its irritation in the zest of creation. 'And the colors are like pink ice cream with cherries in it, or pink stick candy with red stripes.'

They went off in gales of laughter.

'But I say, Harriet,' Johnnie observed, 'wouldn't it be fun to see if she'd look human if we dressed her that way? Couldn't we ——?'

'My, but you're consistent!' Harriet observed. Johnnie pinched her with vigorous fingers.

The next night a hundred pairs of eyes anxiously considered the heavens. The dozen Seniors had gathered on the campus to sing, as was their Friday-night custom. It was one of the soft, mysterious hours when the birds called sleepily and the moon rose red out of the bay and fireflies meshed themselves in the streamers of gray moss that hung like enchanted veils before its ruddy lantern. Voices were full and sweet and mellow, and the world held no unloveliness. And when the whole school joined in the Negro National Anthem, singing from dormitory windows and balconies, Harriet felt her heart climb.

> 'Sing a song full of the faith
> That the dark past has taught us;
> Sing a song full of the faith
> That the present has brought us ...'

Next morning a hundred girls pulled open sleepy eyes when the rising bell rang at half-past six, and dashed to their windows to see whether it was fair. It was.

Saturday was always busy. Girls who were earning their board by extra housework were wielding strenuous brooms and mops and dustcloths. Girls who earned by washing for the faculty must hurry across to Jaynes Hall with their bundles. All the girls had washing and ironing to do for themselves, anyway, unless they had managed to squeeze it in during the week. And it was not easy to do that in odd minutes at Landers, where there was no modern easy way to wash lingerie and hose in rooms or bathrooms.

Harriet and Johnnie and Mossie went flying with the rest, cleaning their rooms, making their beds according to the exact conventions of Landers students, doing their washing, rushing back to their rooms to dress.

Mossie's dark little face was more somber than usual, with a stocking top pulled down to the brows. She had been using pomade on her hair and combing it with a heated iron comb set like a poker in a coiled handle.

'Johnnie,' she asked timidly, 'how y'all keep yo' hair so straight an' shiny?'

'It grew that way.' Johnnie was almost regretful: Mossie had looked so hopeful.

Mossie's lip sagged mournfully.

'Why do you care?' Harriet asked. 'I don't — much. I'll admit it's a nuisance to go to all the bother of straightening it and then have it wind itself up as tight as the dickens the minute a damp breeze hits it. — Especially here, where all the breezes are damp.'

'Oh, well' — Johnnie treated the matter lightly, not being personally annoyed by it — 'did you ever see white girls with their hair all curled just so, and then after they'd been out in the rain and it looked like something the cat had dragged in? — Of course not with permanent waves. But did you ever see them getting their permanent waves? They have their hair all twisted up tight and clamped to the electric light, and there they have to *sit* — anyway in the old-fashioned kind they do — looking like Medusa, for hours on end, no matter how it pulls and burns. And then when the operator undoes it and combs it out, like enough they say, "Horrors! it's just like *wool!*"'

Mossie cringed. Wool was a word she and her friends did not allow in their vocabulary.

Johnnie laughed at her discomfort. 'Why on earth is it so much worse to have to *straighten* your hair than to have to *curl* it?' she demanded.

'Because it is,' Harriet said flatly.

'A fellow's own handicaps are always worse than the other fellow's,' Johnnie jeered.

Mossie, meanwhile, had taken her purple and yellow dress from its hanger. Suddenly she squeaked piteously and held the skirt up to view, a gaping tear in the back.

'That won't be much of a trick to mend,' Johnnie assured her crisply.

'Mend!' Mossie stared at her, face twisted. 'I ain' studyin' de mendin'. Lookit de shape!'

'Why, it's just an ordinary three-cornered tear,' Harriet briskly seconded Johnnie, her voice receding as she lifted her brown-flowered voile over her head and wriggled into it.

'But dis shape, hit bad luck!' Mossie wailed. 'Hit mean a inimy done lay a trap fo' me.'

'Oh, *Mossie!*'

Mossie looked at them as at benighted beings. 'Sho' nuff it do,' she said solemnly.

Here Harriet interrupted. 'Oh, good gracious!' she cried in studied consternation, like a girl speaking a part in a school play. 'I can't have grown so much as this! Kids, would you kindly look at this dress?'

Johnnie grinned behind Mossie's back, and Mossie clasped shocked hands. 'Oh, an' e too pretty!' she squealed. 'Cain' y'all leave down de hem, m'm?'

Harriet shook her head, tugging vainly to bring the

sides of the placket together. Then she blinked and
frowned at Mossie. 'Why, I bet it would be just right for
you!' she cried. 'I wouldn't feel half so bad if it didn't
have to be wasted.'

While Johnnie stuck out her chin and her lower lip to
button her collar, surveying the pair with judicial eyes,
Mossie let the dress drop over her head. 'Why, e do fit!'
she exclaimed.

'Isn't it amazing?' murmured the conspirators, who had
feverishly stitched it by hand, hiding it under Johnnie's
pillow when anyone approached the door.

'I say!' cried Johnnie, snapping thumb and finger.
She whirled into her own room and returned with a cream-
colored ribbon and a pair of brown ankle hose. 'Weren't
these just made to go with that dress?' she crowed, and
tied the ribbon about Mossie's round head with a bow
sitting perkily atop.

Mossie stood on one foot at a time to change her stockings. Her eyes did not swerve from the mirror Harriet
had set on the bed.

'I don' reckon it me a-tall,' she whispered.

At eleven the campusful was packed into trucks and
cars and the last forgotten box of food had been remembered and run back after, and the caravan rolled out along
the black highway toward the 'main.' When they had
crossed the causeway from their island they were in
territory new to Harriet.

They rolled past cabins set in autumn fields, all much
alike and all like Granny's, with a lovely slope of roof from
ridge to front eave of porch. People sat on the rickety
porches, and banana trees ruffled ragged leaves in the
breeze, or chinaberries spread dense shadows, or live-oaks
towered gigantic above the squatting cabins.

They passed between dark cypress swamps and swept
through a ruinous gateway into a magnificent avenue

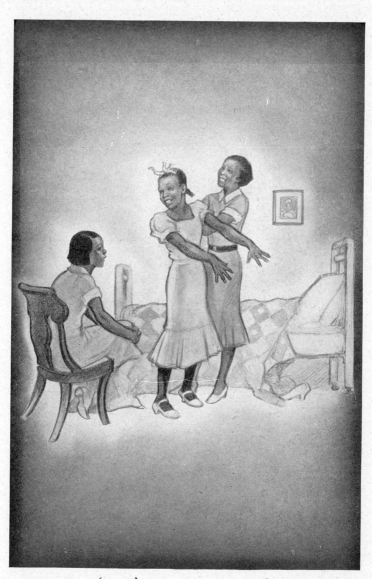

'I DON' RECKON IT ME A-TALL'

of oaks, their branches almost touching the ground and stretching along it fifty feet or more.

'Tolliver,' said Mossie.

'No!' Harriet spoke with a stifled scream. For Taliaferro — she sat erect and stared before her — Taliaferro was the plantation where Black Moses had lived and died.

She had not known that it was the goal of the day's excursion. Eagerly she stared across the broad stretches of tangled grass to the feathery clumps of bamboo through which the river glinted. Here, in an unbelievably far past, her own forebears had lived in slaves' quarters.

The picnic was served cafeteria style on the broad lawn, and when the girls had gathered up their sandwiches and salad and cups of cocoa, they formed groups for eating. Joan Senter — the girls were calling her Miss Joan, now, at her own suggestion — and Mrs. La Rocque, Harriet, Johnnie, and Mossie, made one circle. It was a congenial group, yet Harriet could scarcely keep her mind from the past to savor the present.

'*Qu'est-ce que c'est que ça?* — A penny for your thoughts, child!' Mrs. La Rocque challenged her.

Harriet unkinked her brows and looked embarrassed. 'Do excuse me. I was thinking about my great-great-great grandfather, Black Moses. He was a slave on this very plantation,' she said candidly. 'But I think he must have been a wonderful slave.'

Mossie emerged from her cocoon of silence. 'Tollivers y'all whi' folks?' she demanded. 'Dey us-all, likewise.' She sucked in her breath and stared at Harriet with the hanging lip Harriet so often itched to tap back into place. 'Y'all say *Black Moses?*'

Harriet nodded, wonderingly.

'M'mudder's granny tell 'bout Black Moses. Ever I git 'm mix wif Moses in de Good Book. A'mighty big, dey say, an' a'mighty strong, so e pull up trees wif e's han's when e mad. Y'all mean Black Moses, yo' grampa?'

Mrs. La Rocque laughed. 'Evidently he's become a colored Paul Bunyan, Harriet,' she observed.

She was studying the two girls. Harriet thought she understood that pondering scrutiny. Harriet's ancestors and Mossie's, slaves on the same plantations; and she and Mossie as widely different as any two girls in the world. After all, individuals were individuals.

And what an individual Black Moses must have been! What a personage! Harriet pictured him, a Joseph in the land of the Pharaohs: subject to them; captive; but treated with dignity, with respect, as became his rank in his own land, his personality anywhere.

They all dawdled around the grounds a while, Harriet repeopling it with great ladies and little, hoop-skirted, pantaletted girls and long-trousered boys; and dark faces above white kerchiefs; and dark arms plunged into the morass of the rice field: up — down, up — down, to the rhythm of barbaric chanting. She had to shake herself free from the phantoms of the past when Miss Francis called them to join in the games and races.

The three girls took part with equal reluctance. They probably would not have taken part at all if it had not been for Roseanne Gibbs. She primmed her little mouth and drew so far aloof as to make it clear that she had come to the picnic only because compelled, and *would not* demean herself by playing games. So Harriet and Johnnie stepped resignedly forward in response to the principal's summons, and Mossie, of course, trailed after them.

Mossie's hands shook so that she dropped all her peanuts in the peanut race; and she did not start running in the hundred-yard dash until the others were halfway to the goal. Johnnie sauntered amusedly through the events. But Harriet, though she had not wanted to contest with her hostile schoolmates, could not resist the joy of running when once she had started. She easily broke the day's record in the hundred-yard dash and in the standing jump.

'You actually impressed Willie Lou the Great!' Johnnie drawled. 'She has designs on you — she's captain of the basketball team, you know.'

Yes, Willie Lou was scowling darkly in Harriet's direction, from the center of the group that she had huddled around her for conference.

'I can't imagine that I'd want to play on a little team like this,' Harriet said stiffly.

VIII

WILLIE LOU

HARRIET, Johnnie, and Mossie filed into chapel one after the other. Except for her shoes, Mossie no longer looked as if she had been pulled out of the ragbag. She wore the brown-flowered tan voile everywhere and always, washing and ironing it with scrupulous care every two days.

'I hope to goodness she'll get her new dress done, in sewing class, before that voile is simply washed to pieces,' Harriet said to Johnnie. 'Otherwise I've got to outgrow something more, and she might catch on.'

'That dress has made a heap of difference,' Johnnie agreed. 'She's begun to clasp her arms across her chest now, when she marches, instead of trying to hide her hands somewhere. I think it's one step up from that scared scurry of hers.'

The three girls were still a study in angles. Johnnie, airily erect, sauntered with tailored skirt swinging. Harriet strode like a young goddess in bronze, head thrown back, gaze frowning. Mossie scurried forward and dropped back, round head tucked down, startled eyes rolling, shapeless shoes slapping flatly. She could not sit with the other two: they were in Senior section and she in

Eighth Grade. Separated from them, she sat hunched together as if fearing look or blow. Only when there was a general singing of spirituals was she released from her frightened self-consciousness.

Harriet, too, loved the spirituals, and because of them she liked the chapel hour. It was much like all chapel hours. Girls studied surreptitiously and passed notes and whispered with caution as students do in chapel everywhere. And the talks given by some of them were like those in Young People's meeting in Harriet's home church, when members rose and read from printed slips articles to which no one paid any attention. Here, in addition, the speakers were most of them unused to public appearance: they stood shaking and terrified and repeated their talks in high, breathless voices, having evidently learned them by heart.

Today it was different. Today the speaker was Willie Lou.

Willie Lou took her place on the platform awkwardly and began awkwardly, but her speech was no thing of rote, and it soon caught Harriet's grudging attention. 'The Uplift of Our Race,' Miss Francis had announced the subject; and Willie Lou of the smouldering eyes began like a slow fire that smokes and crackles at first and then leaps into a blaze.

'Some of yo' girls say yo' tired hearin' about race, race, race,' she accused them. 'You know when we gwine get rid of race? When we get rid of thisyere brown skin of ours!' — She thrust out her pale-palmed brown hands — 'What we got to study is how we gwine step up higher!'

She breathed hard, head forward, eyes burning. 'We got to step up higher by holdin' hands and climbin' all together. Hark to me! Every one of us that does something big; every one that writes a book or paints a picture or sings or acts or preaches — big! — we lift the whole

85

race. If we hang together! We don' have to try to be white folks. We aren't white. And colored must be good as white, or why did the Lord make 'em? But long as nine-tenths of our folks live shiftless and know-nothin' in dirty shacks — long as that keeps up the other tenth is held down, too: nine hundred pounds is too big for one hundred pounds to tote on its back. Not if it wants to get anywhere.'

She stood for a moment, hands clenched on the reading desk, chin belligerent. 'It's no use us sayin' the white folks ought to educate us. White folks is a lot of 'em as slack-twisted as colored. And down here most of 'em's dog-poor. You know it. It's up to us to look after our own.'

Her voice rose. 'Quit lookin' to the white folks, I tell you. They don' mind if they did drag us here in the first place. They don' mind if they did take us away from our people and our country. They think it's fine to spend a couple dollars a year to teach a colored child and fifty to teach a white ——'

Before Willie Lou had finished speaking, there were murmurs and even hisses from various parts of the room. The sound was like the wind after the sultry calm that precedes the great storm. It was like flame breaking out from beneath a blanket of smoke.

Harriet looked around her in astonishment. She had not realized that these girls were tinder, ready for the spark, or smouldering flames, ready for the breeze.

Johnnie nudged her, murmuring out of the corner of her mouth: 'This gets bad, sometimes, so the teachers tell Mother. Old grudges flare up and they lose control.'

Harriet's spine crept with uneasiness; but Willie Lou had scarcely sat down when the tall, strongly built Hannah got quietly to her feet.

'Hannah,' asked Miss Francis, 'have you something to add to this spirited talk?'

'Yes, m'm. — I cain' talk like Willie Lou, but I just got to say right here that I agree with her, and I want to thank the white folks that give us a chanct to move up together like Willie Lou says. Startin' way back with Miss Landers who founded thisyere school, right down to Miss Francis and our teachers. *They* ain' never done us any harm. *They* don' owe us an education. I'm glad to God for 'em: they're givin' us all they got. If we use it like we ought to, I reckon we march up together, like Willie Lou say.'

Without a pause, her deep voice swelled out through the room in the spiritual that Harriet loved best:

'Great Day! The righteous marchin'...'

A few at a time, uncertainly, other voices took their answering parts until at length the hundred were gathered in the tide of noble sound. Harriet did not sing: it would be awkward, she felt, to show musical ability where she did not mean to use it; but she listened with a full heart.

'Isn't that Hannah a grand person?' she asked under her breath as they rose. 'All along I've wanted to know her, but she sort of slips out of my way. — Listen! There's hardly any more of a murmur than usual. Hannah turned the trick.'

Hannah had, for the time; but Willie Lou was still simmering. She was still simmering when the Senior girls went swimming in the bay that afternoon.

The swimming instructor was Miss Joan. Harriet and Johnnie enjoyed being with her: she was almost like another girl; there was just enough distance between them to make her friendship a compliment. Harriet was eager for her first plunge in salt water, too.

The campus had its own little beach, so that the girls could put on their swimming suits in their rooms and run through the thicket and down a woodsy path to the water.

Miss Joan, being a teacher, had slipped into a robe which was a silken splash of color.

'It looks more ornamental than useful,' Johnnie objected, contemplating the orange chrysanthemum that bloomed on its back.

'That's what I'm thinking,' Miss Joan agreed. 'I'll hang it up on a hickory limb and not let it near the water.'

The tide was beginning to creep in and swish softly among the rushes. Harriet dashed through shallow water and swam the buoyant waves, Johnnie beside her, until they were well out beyond the group of neophytes.

For a long time they floated on their backs, looking up at the gentle blue of the Carolina sky, across at the columned white mansions of Bosquet.

'Aren't y'all frozen?' chattered Countess Waters from the boat, where she was sunning herself, gray with chill.

They swam over to her. She was a quiet little girl and had always held aloof from them. 'You ought to feel Minnesota water once,' scoffed Harriet, swinging the boat and splashing, while Countess's fingers gripped the gunwale. 'This is too warm if anything. But the only thing I really don't like is having to wear swimming shoes. They make me feel sissy.'

'You sure get your feet cut up with oysters if you don't,' Countess warned, watching admiringly if anxiously.

'I s'pose. Some day I'm going to try it, though. Gosh, isn't this pretty?'

Sweet gum and palmetto marched down to the beach, their green forming a crescent around the cove. Set in that frame the girls were nymphs, old ivory and gold and bronze and ebony.

'I always think we look a lot nicer than white people in bathing suits,' Harriet observed complacently.

'We sure make more noise,' Johnnie said.

The quiet place rang with shrieks, shouts, laughter. Few of the girls could swim — Harriet and Johnnie, Willie Lou and Phyllodoxia. The learners yelled with fear and delight while they balanced frog-like on Miss Joan's palm in the water and jerked inept arms and legs. They yelled with laughter when they stepped into holes. They hooted at each other. When they managed to flounder past their depth and in over their heads they came up blinded and choking and used the first breath from their aching lungs to shriek with merriment. It seemed impossible that so much noise could come from so few girls.

'I always think there's something wrong with one of our people who doesn't laugh easy and laugh a lot,' Johnnie observed, splashing Harriet enthusiastically.

'These South Carolinians are sort of different, though,' said Harriet, unexpectedly grasping Johnnie and holding her under.

'Gosh!' Johnnie spluttered, making fearful noises and blowing water out of mouth and nose.

'And I sometimes wonder whether girls like Willie Lou don't think they're crusaders or something,' Harriet went on, as if there had been no interruption, though she kept out of her companion's reach.

'Willie Lou can laugh hard enough, when there aren't any white people round. It's Ella ——'

Harriet nodded. 'I know. Bitter laughter, hers is. I don't think she's any too good for Willie Lou. — Look, Johnnie. Look at them now.'

Ella and Willie Lou stood where the water curled around their ankles, and watched Miss Joan. Harriet could see the lift and flare of Ella's nostrils, the scornful droop of her eyes. She said something to Willie Lou without turning her head. After a poised instant, Willie Lou gave a shout of laughter and leaped up the slope toward the gum tree where Miss Joan's gay coat was hanging.

'She's up to mischief,' Johnnie said with conviction.

Willie Lou was knotting the sleeves of the soft robe, the body, balling it up in her strong grasp. She took a ball-player's pose and wound up to pitch it toward the bay. But Harriet was moving swiftly, too. Before the bundle had left Willie Lou's hands, Harriet was swimming out to a point which would cross its course, and before it could reach the water her long arm shot up and caught it. With it strained above her head she swam to shore, one corner skimming the waves as she went.

She stamped up the slope and hunched the garment in the fork of a tree until she could shake her hands dry. While she was worrying loose the knots, Miss Joan ran up to her, surprise in her face.

'Why, what happened?' she asked, taking the robe and smoothing it ruefully.

Harriet met Willie Lou's glare evenly. 'I found it that way, Miss Joan. Somebody's idea of a joke.'

'Somebody had a funny idea,' Miss Joan snapped, her color flaming. Willie Lou transferred her glare to the teacher. 'Suppose you joke with my cotton one next time you feel a funny spell coming on,' Miss Joan warned, shaking the rainbow of silk and hanging it up again. 'Now who's next to try that first stroke?'

She ran back into the water, leaving Harriet and Willie Lou to confront each other. Roseanne Gibbs sauntered toward them, languidly curious, her turquoise swimming suit untouched by water. Hannah lingered near, and Countess and Johnnie.

'Teacher's pet!' Ella sneered at Harriet.

'I am not. But you think it's so smart to plague the white teachers. You knew very well it would ruin that robe to get it sopping wet.'

'Shucks! You-all are like babies that are sati'fied with a stick of candy when they've been turnt out of house an' home,' Willie Lou flung at her.

'And *you* remind *me*' — Harriet kindled with the fire of battle — 'of a dog that bites the person who pulls him out from under a car. Sure, somebody ran him down, and if he can't get at the one who hurt him, he'd just as soon take a nip at the one who saved him.'

'I don' think it was ve'y nice, Willie Lou,' Hannah added gently.

IX

BOARDING-SCHOOL BUSINESS

THE next Sunday evening service was in charge of the Seniors. They chose to hold it on the beach, since the weather was fine. Johnnie and Harriet and Phyllodoxia and Countess helped Miss Anthony gather wood for a fire, not to warm the languorous air, but to drive away a few of the millions of hungry mosquitoes. As soon as dusk had fallen, girls and faculty marched in a loose procession across the campus and down the slope. Some of them sat on logs that had been placed out of reach of the tide; most of them stood. Hannah lighted the fire, and it picked out the glint of eyes and teeth from the darkness.

'Hannah,' Miss Anthony asked, 'will you raise "Great Day"?'

Harriet loved the way Hannah 'raised' the spirituals. In chapel she always wanted to turn and watch her. The tall girl sat so serene and relaxed, her hands resting in her lap. When she was asked to lead, her gentle face glowed a little, but she looked aside, shyly, out of the window, and opened her mouth and let her great, sweet voice flow out, strong, quieting.

Tonight her voice was even lovelier than usual. Harriet felt herself carried by the harmony, and before she knew it she was singing herself. There was such beauty in the volume of sound. Even Willie Lou's voice, strident as it was, and Ella's, heavy and husky, added to the pricelessness of the whole.

Miss Anthony repeated, 'The heavens declare the glory of God, and the firmament showeth His handiwork...' Phyllodoxia shyly told a story that she had evidently memorized word for word. In her soft, breathless lisp she gave perfect finish to every sentence, every phrase.

A small breeze turned the smoke toward the log and stung the eyes of the girls there. Along with the lapping of the water and the crackle of the fire there was a gentle slapping of mosquitoes. The salt smell of the bay, the fishy tang, the sharp smell of smoke, the sweet of blossoms, all wove into story and song.

The National Anthem was the climax of the hour. As its stately words rolled out, Harriet forgot everything but the beauty of the night and the sea, and the yearning of her own people. Her round, sweet voice rang out without self-consciousness. When the anthem was ended, she was singing almost alone. Willie Lou's powerful voice and Ella's deep one were not to be heard, and Hannah was humming as if to listen at the same time.

'Good gracious, girl!' Johnnie murmured as they climbed back through the thicket. 'What a voice!'

'Chile!' shouted Deena May, 'that sho' was singin'. I mean *singin'!*'

Study hall was close and bright after the magic outdoors. All the girls in Washington and Douglass Halls were required to study in the largest classroom in the evening. The single small bulbs that dangled nakedly from cords in their cubicles were not bright enough for prolonged reading.

Harriet and Johnnie and Mossie sat in a row, and Harriet often looked up from her solid geometry to watch Miss Bates, the teacher in charge tonight. Harriet liked to study the resignation of that passionate mouth, the sadness of eyes that could light to such a dance of fun.

Now and then Miss Bates walked up and down the aisles to see that her charges were really studying. When Miss Anthony inspected, she folded her arms across her breast, and the dimple that slashed one cheek played in and out as she glanced from desk to desk. Miss Joan strode smartly in her low-heeled oxfords. Miss Bates was different from anyone else: she had a lovely walk; and her hands clasped each other loosely, lightly; and her head was high.

Tonight she stopped at Harriet's side. 'We must have you for the girls' chorus,' she said, nodding gently as she spoke. 'Aren't you ashamed, trying to hide a voice like that?'

Harriet flushed and bent her eyes on her book. Miss Bates didn't resent it, that Harriet had not enrolled with her for piano lessons. Had she heard Harriet practising at Jaynes Hall before breakfast?

The Jaynes Hall piano was not notably good, but Harriet was learning to love that morning hour. The campus was so still; trees and flowers were so watchful; and the sun came up so red out of the bay behind the industrial hall. Sometimes Mossie crept after her and sat huddled at the foot of the stair that led to the second floor. She was a strange audience, Mossie, with her feet toed in and her elbows on her knees and her fists punched into her cheeks while her big eyes wondered at Harriet's swift fingers.

Sometimes Harriet turned with a half-vexed laugh. 'Mossie, I don't see how you can *stand* listening to these scales and exercises.'

'Likes to watch yo' fingers,' Mossie mumbled. 'Likes to hear the soun's come so fas' and — and bright.'

'Listen to this, if you've got to be listening.'

94

Harriet improvised what was in her mind: still islands with lipping waves; the coming of storm; the scream of dying trees; the rain; peace. She looked round at Mossie. Mossie sat with lip fallen and eyes bewildered.

'It isn't any good,' said Harriet.

Now she wondered whether Miss Bates had heard her working on the Prelude in F, on the Moonlight Sonata, and had understood that Harriet couldn't waste her time with a two-dollar-a-month piano teacher who taught humped-over girls like Ella to play 'Lightly Row.'

Ella and Willie Lou were glancing at Harriet now and then. They did not usually come to study hall, but tonight they bent above their books with absorption, except when they covertly studied Harriet. Perhaps they disliked her still more, now that they had found she had a good singing voice.

In spite of them, this had been a pleasant evening, and the three companions loitered over to Washington Hall in a state of unusual contentment. Harriet lingered at Johnnie's door, the two laughing and talking. Mossie went on along the corridor, but she came hurrying back, round-eyed.

'Lawdy, Hayet!' she gibbered, 'y'all better come see what happen!' She twitched at Harriet's sleeve, scurried ahead of her, looked back at her, like a puppy trying to lead its master.

The two other girls were at the door in a moment. Confusion greeted them. The bedding had been jerked from Harriet's cot and tied by its corners into a huge, ungainly bundle which filled the space between the beds. The curtains had been tied in a series of knots. The pictures of Harriet's father and mother, of Helen and Iva and Jimmie, had been taken down and pinned on the wall again upside down. Harriet's suitcases sprawled open and empty on the dismantled cot.

'My — land!' gasped Harriet.

Johnnie stepped briskly over the bundle and undid the knots. Lingerie and nightclothes, costume jewelry, powder and cream, all manner of odds and ends that had been stored in the suitcases were heaped in a wild conglomeration.

'Mighty fine thorough job of stacking a room,' Johnnie commended dryly, as she began to lay the articles in place again.

'Done spill yo' powdah into yo' golden slippahs!' Mossie mourned, squatting on the other side of the heap. 'Done spill all yo' elegant perfume!'

'Stacking a room?' asked Harriet.

'Oh, I forgot you've never been to boarding-school before. Stacking a room is one of the intellectual pursuits of Betty Co-Ed. It's also a lovely way to get even in a light-hearted, girlish fashion. And when there's more in the room more can be accomplished. Such as emptying all the dresser drawers. — I wonder where Willie Lou got the idea?'

'Willie Lou?'

Bestriding the bundle, Johnnie shot Harriet a caustic glance. 'Don't be a poll parrot,' she advised. 'Surely you see Willie Lou's fine hand in all this. The criminal hasn't bothered Mossie. Also, Willie Lou was not down at the beach when we — when you — sang the Anthem.'

Mossie scuttled out into the hall, and Harriet leaped across her household goods to turn her pictures right side up. She snorted. 'I guess I can put up with tricks as well as the next one. — Only she hadn't any business touching Daddy and Mother.'

They had only begun to sort out the medley, a crowd of stocking caps and bathrobes offering suggestions, when a tap sounded at the open door, and Miss Francis's even voice: 'Well, well, young ladies!' Her nostrils were dilated.

and no wonder; the room reeked with lavender toilet water.

Harriet jumped up, anxiously untying the knots in her best chiffon hose and inspecting them to see if the rough handling had pulled their threads. 'Won't you come in, Miss Francis?' she stammered.

'Where?' Miss Francis asked — 'But I've brought you some help.' She motioned Willie Lou to come in. 'This isn't exactly my idea of Landers recreation, Willie Lou.'

Willie Lou glared at Harriet and mumbled something that carried an unmistakable sting of 'tattle-tale' at the end.

'Why, I never!' Harriet exclaimed indignantly, falling back on a childhood phrase.

Miss Francis had caught the muttered word, too. She turned back. 'No, Willie Lou. Harriet told me nothing.'

Under Miss Francis's arm peeped the round eye and dropped lip of Mossie, breathing hard.

'And I haven't the least complaint to make, Miss Francis,' Harriet said firmly, scowling at Mossie. 'Don't they always stack rooms at boarding-schools?'

Willie Lou lingered after Miss Francis had gone.

'There were two dresses you forgot to tie knots in, Willie Lou,' Harriet complained. 'And you're so good at knots.'

Johnnie snickered, a long, hissing giggle between her teeth. Somehow this time they were all laughing, except Willie Lou; and she wasn't there.

When the campus was still, that night, three girls in bathrobes crept out of the front door of Washington Hall. The buildings stood darkened, except for entrance lights and a bright window in the middle of Sarah B. — Miss Francis's window. Crickets chanted, and whippoorwills called mournfully.

The two girls were hurrying a third between them. 'I ain' done nothin',' she whimpered. 'I ain' mean nothin'.'

'Keep your little mouth tight shut for once!' Johnnie ordered.

Across the campus they hurried her, keeping in the shadows because the moon shone full and limpid. They rushed her through the thicket and down the slope and across the strip of sand, because the tide was out. The moonlight made an enchanting scene here, etching itself in the pools among the rushes.

The girls did not take time to look, but for a minute they stopped to listen. Did it come across the waters of the bay, that lovely, eerie sound? Was it sound, or was it a dream?

A phrase came clearly, a delicate march of notes — Bach. A Bach fugue. Harriet stood tranced until the music had been taken into the great orchestra of the night.

'Come on! We've got work to do,' she said.

Straight out across the wet sand they marched.

'Wha' y'all gwine do wid me?' begged Mossie.

'Do you want to gang up with us or don't you?' Harriet queried sternly.

'Sho' — sho' does.'

'Then it's high time you learned that our gang doesn't tattle. We settle our differences in more adult ways.'

They shucked off her robe and rolled up their pajamas; they made a chair of their hands and commanded her to sit on it; they walked out till they were knee-deep in the cool water.

'One for the money,' said Johnnie.

'Two for the show,' said Harriet.

'Three to make ready,' said Johnnie.

'And — four — to — *go!*' said Harriet.

Simultaneously they ducked their heads from under Mossie's encircling arms and unclasped their hands.

Splash went the water, sending silver rings widening —
widening ——

And back to Washington Hall presently dripped three
girls, arm in arm.

X

In the Library

'ANYWAY,' Johnnie commented, 'it makes Willie Lou seem just a spiteful, malicious girl. I thought you were a little off, calling her a crusader. The robe business, and then stacking the room; why, she's just childish.'

'Oh, well, we're all kind of childish,' Harriet said fairly. 'And as for the crusader business, isn't it sort of mixed up together? I shouldn't wonder if Willie Lou considers us traitors to a sacred cause.'

Willie Lou 'made Harriet mad.' She made her see red. Yet she could not help admiring Willie Lou's spirit and determination. Willie Lou, probably coming from a shack that held no printed page except those that papered its walls — Willie Lou, struggling up out of shanty schools and illiterate speech — Willie Lou saw visions and made her companions see them.

'But how can she help knowing that Miss Francis and Miss Joan and the others give up heaps for us all?' Johnnie fumed.

They were on their way to the old cottage which had been the home of Rachel Landers seventy-five years ago and which now housed the sewing-rooms. Here Joan

Senter was poking about in a barrel and hissing a thoughtful tune through her teeth.

'Oh. You two,' she observed when Harriet and Johnnie came in. 'Maybe you can lend me your alleged brains. I want a project, good, big, and different.'

'Expect it to pop out of the barrel, Miss Joan?' inquired Johnnie, swinging one leg from the corner of the table.

'Out of this barrel if at all,' Miss Joan assented. She dragged forth a wire lampshade frame, a stack of oilcloth samples, a mass of embroidery floss, hopelessly tangled, a swatch of tulle which crackled into a dozen breaks, like a handful of autumn leaves, when she shook it free of its folds.

'Where on earth does that junk come from?' Harriet asked, prodding with a gingerly finger. 'Look at this backless formal, would you?'

'It comes from up North. Landers simply hasn't money for Home Ec materials.'

Harriet snorted at the oilcloth samples. 'What under the shining sun could anybody do with those?'

'Oh, my. That shows how dumb you are' — the young teacher cherished them in her hands. 'These are easy. They'll make grand pot-holders to sell in the student store or the Carnival.'

'And the gunny sacks?'

'We *ask* for gunny sacks. Look, Harriet!' She pointed at a row of garments on hangers: a wine-colored dress, a small boy's suit, and another dress of hunter's green; all were of a material that suggested homespun.

Harriet twitched her brows at them. 'What's the connection, Miss Joan?'

Miss Joan jabbed a dramatic finger at them, at the gunny sacks. 'Product and source. Washed, ripped, dyed, cut, sewed, and there you are!'

'Gracious! That's what Mossie's brown and old-gold dress is? Miss Joan, you're a wonder.'

Miss Joan nodded abstractedly, picking up a comb that had flipped out of her curled topknot and thrusting it in again, while one arm went on probing in the depths of the barrel. 'Look at this,' she exclaimed, coming up with a stack of folded cretonne.

'Curtains? Somebody's whole sun parlor,' Johnnie guessed.

Miss Joan unfolded one and held it admiringly at arm's length. 'Not even faded!' she said gloatingly. 'Here's my Home Ec project in a nutshell!'

'How do you mean?' Harriet asked, tilting her head at the red and yellow flowers and the blue parakeets.

'The kitchen!' Miss Joan exploded the word at them, her small chin round with satisfaction. 'You know what the kitchen looks like.'

They did. Both had had to take their turn waiting on tables, and they had grown familiar with the huge, clean room. It was a giant room, with work-tables down the center and a giant stove and cupboards. Always in order, and always smelling pleasantly of fresh bread and meat and vegetables, it was gray and prisonlike, with its drab walls and furniture.

'Curtains would brighten it a lot,' Johnnie agreed.

'Mmmmm!' Miss Joan pounded the pile of cretonne. 'Dutch curtains, cute as a bug's ear. But that isn't all. Jersey-cream-colored walls. Furniture enameled Chinese red. The tin pails they get canned fruit in, and the lard cans and all such, painted cream and lettered for all sorts of supplies. — I think the school will allow us enough to buy paint and enamel,' she said jubilantly. 'And it exactly fits in with our section on interior decoration.'

During the succeeding class period, Harriet could see the kitchen project buzzing behind the young teacher's eyes. Sometimes it popped out of her mouth. — 'That buttonhole's puckered like a drawstring, Harriet. Didn't you ever learn buttonholes? See: like this.' — She took the doll's pajama coat that Harriet was working on. 'I think maybe it will be better to paint the containers first, so as to work the girls up to the walls by degrees.'

'Up is right,' Harriet agreed, frowning over her buttonhole. 'Those walls must be twelve feet high.'

Johnnie was making pajamas for herself, smart affairs with dizzy diagonal stripes. Willie Lou had been dissuaded from an especially violent plaid — Willie Lou was broad as well as tall — and beguiled to choose a print with shaded blue and orange stripes, up and down.

'Johnnie,' Miss Joan suggested, 'if you'd baste more you'd rip less.'

'I like an unstudied effect,' Johnnie objected.

Miss Joan smiled, and Willie Lou looked at them as if they were speaking a strange language.

'It would be pretty to line the curtains with flame color — there are so many gray days,' said Miss Joan; 'if we could afford it!'

Harriet had a free period after Home Economics, and she went into the library to do some collateral reading for her history class. That history class — Negro History, it was — made her think of the quotation about a liberal education — Mark Hopkins on one end of a log and the student on the other. Any log would be a grand school, Harriet thought, with Miss Francis on it. Harriet had always found history dull and lifeless. Now it was alive and absorbing. It even challenged her to do extra reading.

But the library did depress her. Back of its gray wood floors and pine tables always floated the tiles and waxed oak of other libraries she had known. Back of its meager shelves of books, most of them old books, glowed the well-filled stacks and huge card catalogues of Minneapolis. Here she felt the full contrast between past surroundings and present.

And today Willie Lou accented the contrast. Unspeaking, she had tramped along behind Harriet. Unspeaking, she sat down opposite her, opened a book, and rested her forehead studiously on her hands.

Ten minutes, fifteen, the two girls sat there. Harriet doubted whether Willie Lou had turned a single page. She herself read and turned pages to the end of a chapter, and then turned back to begin over again, her mind a blank. She looked across the table. Willie Lou dropped her hands to her chin and returned the look.

Willie Lou cleared her throat and asked angrily, 'Did y'all ever play basketball? The girls want I should ask yo' to come to practice. Y'all run good — an' yo' got plenty muscle.'

Harriet laughed nervously.

'Well,' she said, 'I don't know — When is practice?'

'You-all ever play?' Willie Lou repeated. 'We got a right good team. Don' need baby players.'

Harriet's face grew hot. This was one of the times when the other girl's insolence sent all her nerves hopping with anger. 'I played forward on a Centennial team. Centennial had only two thousand girls to draw from,' she said coldly.

'Why'n't you go back to yo' two thousand?' Willie Lou sneered. 'You-all sure don' fit in here so good. Why'n't you go back to yo' swell father and mother dressed up in their silks and di'monds? Why did they send you-all pokin' round to spy on us, anyways?'

Harriet's lonesomeness, her homesickness, seemed to flood over her in a great tide of pain at Willie Lou's taunting words. Her eyes were hot and she felt sick at her stomach.

'Don't you — don't you dare speak of my mother and father like that. It was a hateful trick to turn their pictures upside down. It was a low, mean thing to do!' she raged, leaning across the table to blaze into Willie Lou's face. 'They were the best father and mother that ever lived! They were the dearest ——'

Her head went down on her arms with a bump and she was crying; not silent, dignified weeping, but loud, hiccupping sobs, like a little child's.

She felt arms across her shoulders. She heard a deep, slow voice asking, '*Were?* Y'all ain' say "were"?'

She could do nothing but sob.

A gentle hand rested on her head. 'Y'all mean "were," honey?' the voice persisted.

Harriet bobbed her head a little.

'Last year — Mother——' she managed to stammer. 'Father — years ago. — Nobody in the world — but Granny — over on Gentlemen's Island ——'

'No kin but her Granny, over on Gentlemen's,' the deep voice relayed her words. 'Why, chillen, she's nothin' but a po' little drift. Fine clothes don' count — Why, honey ——'

The room had grown still. Harriet could hear nothing but her own sobs. She fumbled for her handkerchief and poked at her hidden face with it. At length she sat up, wishing that the floor would swallow her.

Girls were bent over books, tensely silent. Girls stood hunched before bookshelves. Close on one side of Harriet sat Hannah. Close on the other side sat Willie Lou.

'It — it might make y'all feel better to get out and practise on the team this evenin',' Willie Lou said gruffly.

XI

Paint Sandwiches

It was fun to play basketball again. Rules were different: Centennial used girls' rules, Landers boys'. Harriet soon grew accustomed to the change.

Johnnie and Mossie both tried out, because Harriet did. Johnnie was no player, and at first Mossie was worse. But gradually she developed something. She was small and elusive. She had a way of ducking and sliding and scurrying so that she never was where you thought she was going to be. Willie Lou said she might make a right good runnin' center if she didn't grow too much.

'Ain' gwine grow no mo',' Mossie confided to Harriet. 'Done tote too many heavy washin's fo' Mammy. I'm close on seventeen now.'

Harriet scrutinized the little creature in shocked surprise. In basketball bloomers and middy Mossie had more than ever the goblin look of Lily, the Drift.

Yet now, dressed alike, the girls seemed less alien to Harriet. Under the swaying ribbons of moss, shrieking like young savages and leaping and whirling and running in the game, they were all — just girls, whether they had come from Minneapolis or Jamaica, from New York, like

Phyllodoxia, from Charleston, like Roseanne, from Green Corners, like Mossie, from Dafuskey, like Willie Lou.

The other girls seemed to regard Harriet more as a human being, also. They had even elected her vice-president of the class in place of Lizzie Gill, called home by illness. That was almost immediately after the episode in the library. Hannah proposed her name and Countess seconded it, and Harriet felt that the vote was carried because she, Harriet, was 'nothing but a poor little drift.' — She would never have anything to do, since Willie Lou was president. Still, she did like being a class officer.

She was altogether happier. She began to feel as she had in Minneapolis, as if each separate twig on every tree she met had an especially joyous message for her; as if every smell and sight and sound were for her, personally; as if she would like to dance on tiptoe instead of walking; and as if she could eat twice as much as was on the table. In fact, she began to feel natural. She decided that it was outdoor exercise that had made the change: in fair weather basketball practice was always outdoors.

Basketball was not her only exercise: Miss Joan's kitchen project provided extra activity and promised more. As soon as the quick-drying enamel came, an evening was given to transforming cupboards and tables and stools, all the Junior and Senior girls convening the minute the supper dishes were done, and working in shifts. Miss Francis even let the last shifts work past the bedtime bell, while the ghosts of earlier shifts, in bathrobes and stocking nightcaps, watched their progress with giggles and murmured encouragement and criticism, skittering up the back stairs when their scouts gave warning of approaching teachers.

An end of the gingerbready porch of the Home Ec cottage was fenced off with chairs, too, and carpeted with newspapers as a workshop. Here the girls painted containers and lettered them. In sewing classes they made the cretonne curtains, lining them with flour sacks dyed orange 'to make a sunshine on a cloudy day'; and hemmed other sacks for dishtowels, cross-stitching them in gay designs.

In other Home Economics class-hours Harriet was working diligently on doll clothes, since Miss Joan agreed that they offered good practice. Harriet had measured the first garments and sent the size to Mrs. Trindle, and in early November the desired doll came to fit them: a cunning, long-legged little girl with bobbed yellow hair. The girls flocked round Harriet when she unwrapped it, exclaiming as they passed it from hand to hand. They all liked dolls.

Not that they played with them; but, as other girls in schools and colleges in other parts of the country have had Kewpies on their dressers, or limber-legged French dolls and grotesque cloth elephants and dogs among the fluffy cushions on their beds, so the Landers girls had dolls.

A Landers bed was made according to strict rule. The spread was laid smoothly over the sheets, and the quilts and blankets rolled or folded in neat patterns on top of the spread. And sitting against these rolls or squares or triangles were dolls.

Willie Lou was the only girl who did not admire Harriet's doll without reservation.

'Oh, Lawdy!' she said, rotating it. 'Buckruh (white) doll, just like the rest. Looks like we could have our doll-babies colored. Looks like when we draw pictures of us fo' the school paper we could anyways make us look tanned. No suh! Ev'y one of those gals we draw is lily-white. And ev'y one of them doll-babies is buckruh.'

She thrust the doll brusquely at Harriet. Harriet had some sympathy with Willie Lou's viewpoint; she had rather admired Willie Lou's round brown little doll, the only dark one she had seen at Landers. And she didn't resent the brusqueness: Willie Lou was cross because she was having 'the shakes.'

Harriet was anxious about the shakes. Willie Lou had had several attacks of malaria since she had come back to school in September, and each attack was a threat to the big game with Booker, scheduled for the last Saturday in November. So much depended on Willie Lou.

And not only in basketball was she important this fall. The Seniors were in charge of the Carnival, which was billed for the third Saturday, and Willie Lou was president of the Senior Class. Her malaria gave the whole school 'the shakes.'

On the second Saturday, she and Harriet were assigned, together with Roseanne Gibbs and Phyllodoxia, to paint one wall of the kitchen, Miss Joan having determinedly shuffled the usual cliques. A wall at a time was as much as the best-natured of cooks — Miss Mitty — could be expected to endure.

Roseanne and Phyllodoxia had been deputed for the part below the chair rail and Willie Lou and Harriet, both tall and agile, for the part above. They mixed the yellow paint out in the graveled space behind the kitchen, and divided it into four coffee cans. That is, three of them mixed and divided, while Roseanne looked down her nose and curled her lip at the process.

'I don't call this any Home Ec project,' she said haughtily.

'I call it a swell one,' Harriet retorted.

'Wisht I could paint up my own mother's house so bright and pretty,' Countess said wistfully from the doorway.

Roseanne led the way in, nostrils dilated. 'Where do I begin?' she asked languidly.

'Begin where you darn please!' Harriet snapped. But she cut off with a laugh the further remarks that crowded to her lips: Roseanne looked so funny in her borrowed suit of coveralls, her Lady Vere de Vere manner sticking up out of a rough-dried denim bib. 'You and Doxy can settle that,' Harriet added more amiably.

So Roseanne began in one corner and leaned forward at an angle of forty-five degrees and lifted a dripping brush from her coffee can.

'Golly, gal!' shouted Ella, stacking clean dishes in a cupboard. 'Gwine have that yeller paint all over the floor, and Miss Mitty skin you alive!'

Hannah, who also worked in the kitchen, twisted to see, while she wrung out a soapy dishcloth. Then she loped across the room with a newspaper she jerked from its storage place. 'Spread'm down good and thick, honey,' she advised, and then spread them herself. Roseanne watched from under the drooping lids of one who does a service in letting herself be served.

Meanwhile Phyllodoxia had scurried to place newspapers in her own corner, and now she began to draw the wet brush across the lead-gray wall in luscious, creamy strokes. Harriet and Willie Lou dragged a long table over against the wall, set two chairs on it, laid a plank across the chairs.

'Golly!' Ella observed. 'Y'all better make haste. Miss Senter won' like you go climbin' thataway.'

'It's perfectly all right if we keep balanced,' Harriet argued.

'Only way to reach thisyere high old wall,' Willie Lou grumbled, 'without we totes those heavy old ladders clean across the campus.'

She climbed on the plank first and balanced there, holding the can of paint in one hand and dipping the brush daringly.

'Whee!' squealed Countess Waters, cutting great loaves of homemade bread for the day's picnic and spreading them with peanut butter. 'Willie Lou, you-all mind what you're doing, or you eat paint sandwiches today.'

'I sho' got the shakes,' Willie Lou admitted. 'But you mix the paint up good with that grunnet butter and I won't mind.'

Harriet reached as high as she could and flowed a rich ribbon of color from her brush. She glanced appraisingly down at Roseanne's corner. Not so good. How could Roseanne make every brush stroke show, skimpy and stringy? Miss Joan had warned them to try to make one coat do; paint, she reminded them, cost money.

'Sort of flow it on, Roseanne,' Harriet advised.

Roseanne threw her a brief glance and went on without reply.

The four girls painted, and Hannah washed dishes and sang, and Countess made sandwiches and hummed, and Miss Mitty took from the oven pans of hot bread, which she set on a cupboard ledge almost under Harriet's nose. The savory steam rose to the top of the room and made Harriet swallow hungrily. Wouldn't a heel of that bread taste good, hot and a little soggy from being cut too soon, and soaked with butter?

'You've done your half of the high part, Willie Lou,' she said, staring at the loaves. 'Now let me do mine.'

'Just as lief,' said Willie Lou. 'Got the shakes so bad.'

Harriet had covered all but a square foot of her portion when Willie Lou, glancing over her shoulder, hissed, 'Jiggers, Hayet!'

Harriet looked at her inquiringly.

'Miss Senter. She gwine skin you, climbin' like that.'

Harriet slapped her brush convulsively down the decreasing gray rectangle. Again. Again.

'Mind the plank!' Willie Lou exclaimed, and her hand shot out toward it.

Harriet had no chance to mind anything. Just as she caught sight of Miss Joan's disapproving face, she felt the plank jarring from under her feet. Down to the table she came crashing, clutching can and brush as if they could save her. From the table to the floor she bumped, the paint making a geyser as she went.

'Harriet Freeman!' cried Miss Joan, darting in from the door.

'My fresh bread!' moaned Miss Mitty. 'Hope y'all ain' killed, honey!'

'Hayet, if you fix yo'se'f so you cain' play in the Booker game ——' howled Willie Lou.

Harriet dazedly felt of herself and shook her head. A thick stream trickled down her nose, feeling gruesome and gory. She wiped a hand across it. It was bright yellow instead of red.

'How on earth —— ?' Miss Joan demanded.

'Willie Lou pushed the plank,' Roseanne Gibbs remarked coolly.

Willie Lou's mouth fell open. 'My land, let me ketch you once, you little old ——' she stuttered.

Harriet looked quickly at Willie Lou, and the girl's eyes met hers squarely, holding them with a question that was at once defiant and anxious.

'Don't be silly, Roseanne,' Harriet said definitely. 'Willie Lou did no such thing. — I don't think I'm broken,' she added seriously. She looked at the loaf of bread beside her, on which, in some unexplained way, her hand had been planted. 'If I took off the top paint,' she said, 'it would still taste good, with butter.'

'Well,' said Miss Joan, 'you're going to have to take off some of the top paint from yourself — with turpentine and a bath. We're due to start on that picnic in an hour.'

'Anyway,' said Harriet, gingerly gathering herself together and getting up, 'our wall's painted.'

Countess, showing all her little white teeth in a smile, broke off the painty top crust of the bread and scraped the under crust, which had come in contact with the floor when Harriet's wideflung hand struck it. With a shy, 'Please, m'm, Miss Mitty?' and a glance under her lashes at the cook, she buttered the squashed loaf and held it out to Harriet.

'Won't some of you share it with me?' Harriet invited; 'Countess? Hannah? Ella?'

Everyone refused with thanks, and Harriet alternately munched and cleaned up her part of the painty mess. It was fortunate the linoleum had been well papered. Harriet wadded up the yellow-splashed paper and Hannah opened the range for her to crowd it in.

Presently she was walking across the campus with Miss Joan, Harriet consuming the rest of the loaf as she went. It *was* good, even though most of the crust had been lost.

'You'll not have any appetite for the picnic,' the teacher protested.

'Watch me!' Harriet replied thickly. 'I've got a whale of an appetite, Miss Joan. I never do get filled up.'

'That's always the way with girls in boarding-school,' said Miss Joan, smiling as reminiscently as if her girlhood had been past for twenty years.

The smile faded, however, and she studied Harriet with an uncomfortably cool keenness in her gray eyes. 'I really am disappointed,' she reproved. 'But perhaps I expected too much of you. I didn't suppose I needed to be on guard this morning to see that you didn't do anything foolish. That was my mistake. And if one of you had been injured by that silly stunt of a plank on two chairs on a table — well, I'd have been liable in all sorts of ways.'

Harriet threw the last quarter of her loaf into a clump

of bushes. It didn't taste so good. She walked beside Miss Joan, hot and miserable. Sometimes it took just that much to dash one's spirits to the ground. Miss Joan's disapproval shed a sudden, clear, cold light on the painting episode and made it look silly and childish.

'I'm sorry, Miss Joan,' she muttered. She wasn't good at expressions of repentance. 'But I do think I'm punished enough without your looking at me like that,' she added with a rush. 'You may think it's fun to come smashing down every which way. I feel like a dozen eggs and all of them scrambled. — I beg your pardon for speaking that way,' she added, remembering that this was, after all, a teacher.

Miss Joan laughed and peered at Harriet's battered elbow. 'You come right straight into my room and get that thing disinfected and dressed,' she said.

XII

THE CARNIVAL

BY THE middle of October the Carnival had been adver-
tised with posters in Booker and the high schools of
Bosquet and Yemassee and even Charleston and Savannah.
It was always one of the biggest social events of the Landers year.

Harriet was listed on the committee of arrangements,
but only because she was an officer in the class, she knew.
With Willie Lou in control, Harriet had nothing to do
with plans or preparations; she had only to plan her own
costume for the evening.

At first she had thought of representing Black Moses;
but there was no telling who might come — from Booker,
for instance; and in case anyone important was there,
Harriet didn't really want to be playing the part of a man.
So she decided to be Harriet Tubman, leader of her own
race, and she studied histories and novels of the period
for costume, and rooted through the odds and ends in
the attic of Sarah B. for materials with which to concoct
the quaint outfit.

To the attic of Sarah B. had been taken the most
fantastic offerings from the barrels sent to Mather: old

silk hats too dilapidated for selling in the Sales House, old party gowns, old canes, split umbrellas, odd gloves; besides contributions by generations of teachers and girls. After its decades of slow growth the collection was an amazing one. Harriet and Johnnie and Mossie reveled in their search, there under the eaves. Harriet and Johnnie soused their finds thoroughly in gasoline and aired them in the drying yard down behind Jaynes Hall, and Mossie imitated their fastidious care, though with the round eyes and dropped lip of bewilderment.

But Harriet was not to slip through the Carnival so easily. On Wednesday Miss Francis stopped her as she passed the faculty table after dinner.

'Harriet,' she said, in the soft, light voice which nevertheless held so much decisiveness — periods where periods should be — 'you are vice-president of the Senior Class.'

'Yes, Miss Francis.'

'Willie Lou is down with a really bad attack of malaria. You will have to take charge of the Carnival in her place.'

'Oh, Miss Francis!' Harriet protested, drawing down her brows. 'The girls only elected me vice-president because — well, they happened to be feeling sorry for me just then. I don't know but they felt sorrier for themselves when they'd calmed down.'

'Still, you are vice-president.'

'But it's only three days before the Carnival ——'

'Willie Lou had everything planned and moving. In the morning you can go to the infirmary and find out what she has done and what there is to do.'

But in the morning Harriet could find out nothing. 'Willie Lou's clean out of her head,' the nurse said, turning Harriet and Johnnie away from the door. 'We haven't had such a hard case in years.'

'I suppose we've got to ask that Ella where Willie Lou kept her notes,' Harriet said. 'Maybe I'll get a chance to do *some*thing that hasn't been done every year since the Civil War,' she added, brightening.

'Go easy, gal,' Johnnie advised lightly. 'You've been doing pretty well; don't upset the apple-cart.'

'Hm?' Harriet asked abstractedly.

'The cook doesn't like to have the caller come into the kitchen and tell her what seasonings to use.'

'Hm?' Harriet repeated. 'Oh, there's Ella. — Ella, where did Willie Lou keep her programs and arrangements and things? Notes, you know, about the Carnival?'

'She didn't keep notes,' said Ella. 'Reckon you-all got to fire ahead best you can. You're vice-president,' she conceded sourly.

'I guess I'd better give out a notice in chapel this morning,' Harriet planned, 'telling the committees to report after dinner. And everyone who's on the program.'

'Likewise the girls who've got charge of the booths and things,' Ella suggested unwillingly.

The announcement brought Roseanne, who was to sing, Phyllodoxia, who was to give a reading, and Countess, who was to have charge of the Chamber of Horrors. It brought also the managers of booths and other concessions.

'Why, this isn't going to be near enough of a program!' Harriet exclaimed, her brows fierce. 'Why, with people coming from as far as Charleston, we can't have a measly little program ——'

'We don't need such a great of a program,' Ella said resentfully, 'with the candy booth and the grunnet (peanut) booth and' — She ticked off a half-dozen attractions, bending back the long flexible fingers of one hand with a finger of the other — 'you-all give folks too much pieces and music and they don' get time to buy. Maybe it ain' thataway up No'th.'

Harriet gave scant attention to Ella's lowering face

and to the uneasy silence of the others. 'Wouldn't it be nice if we could have something striking and distinctive?' she asked eagerly. 'A waffle booth, maybe, with cane sirup and somebody dressed up with a white kerchief. Or a fried fish booth. Or maybe this benny candy.' Benny candy was a crisp rich with bene or sesame seeds instead of nuts. — Harriet was picturing how anyone who happened to come from Gentlemen's Island would admire her ability and originality if the evening sparkled with new and amusing features.

'But thisyere's Wednesday,' Countess reminded her timidly. 'There isn't time to change ev'ything, Harriet. And where'd we get waffle irons enough?'

'But how shall we fill in the whole evening?' Harriet persisted.

'There's the Grand March, so the visitors can see all the costumes,' Countess went on.

'And we can use a heap of time singin',' Hannah offered. 'And we always have singin' games fo' ev'ybody.'

'Singing games?'

'Like Git About Cindy, and String Them Beans. Ev'ybody knows 'em. We always play 'em.'

'That's it: you've played them forever!' Harriet exclaimed. 'This time let's have something brand new!'

Johnnie drummed her chair arm and hummed something under her breath and Ella and Deena May shuffled their feet noisily, but Harriet went on thinking.

'A scavenger hunt!' She exploded the words.

Johnnie chuckled ironically.

'Scag — ?' Countess murmured.

'We'd make out lists of things the people had to find, and of course in this case we'd have to hide them around Jaynes Hall.'

'What kind of things?' Ella demanded.

'Well, I remember one where we had to find a pair of

ear muffs and a mustache cup. — But we'd have to do it quite differently for the Carnival.'

'My father's got a mustache cup,' Hannah said in some perplexity. 'But he ain' got any mustache.'

'*Ear* muffs?' squealed Deena May. 'What you-all mean, ear muffs?'

'You think you-all can make our folks understand how you mean?' Countess asked, her soft little face troubled.

'Oh, that's easy!' Harriet waved away the difficulty with an enthusiastic hand. 'And think what fun it will be to have a change for once! Johnnie, you and Doxy and — and Roseanne can help with the lists.'

'Well,' said Johnnie, after a look at the blankly unresponsive faces about them, 'it's your funeral, Harriet.'

Harriet was too well pleased with her idea to notice. 'Who plays for the solo and the community singing and the Grand March?' she asked.

'Miss Bates does.'

'And who tends to decorating the hall?'

'Chairman does. — *You* do.'

'Well — maybe Miss Senter will take us out in her car early Saturday morning. I think loads of Spanish moss — And how about a big orange moon showing through a fringe of the moss? — What do you think, Ella?' Ella's throat-clearings and shufflings had at last pierced her absorption.

'Me? I don' have to think!' Ella rumbled. 'You-all can do the thinkin' for the lot of us.'

Harriet stared at her. 'One other thing,' she said icily. 'Wouldn't it be fun to sort of exhibit Miss Senter's kitchen project that night? Like a housewarming? What would you suggest, Countess?'

Countess looked up and down and smoothed her dress.

'You-all might put on a stunt,' Ella said, 'showin' how nice you can land in a loaf of light-bread.'

'We do have housewarmin's for new houses,' Countess said. 'Soon as the house is built, we ask all the folks and we sing and pray all night and have eats in the mornin'. — Maybe we could make the Grand March from Jaynes's to the kitchen ——'

'Then round the kitchen till they've all seen it,' Harriet agreed.

'What would you have for music?' asked Johnnie.

'When we got no fiddle, neither banjo, we just beat on the wall with a stick.'

'Ella,' Harriet asked determinedly, 'will you take full charge of the kitchen-warming? — Phyllodoxia, will you check up on the booths and see that they're going to be decorated and ready? It looks to me,' she finished complacently, 'as if things were going to go all right in spite of malaria.'

There were no more hitches than a school party has to have in order to be a school party. Harriet and Johnnie and Phyllodoxia and Roseanne labored till all hours on their scavenger hunt, typing two hundred lists and hiding innumerable objects throughout the hall after it had been decorated. Harriet was only vaguely discomfited by the grudging response of the Senior Class in general: she had too much to do to notice the atmosphere.

Saturday was rainy; all afternoon it drizzled and by dinnertime a heavy downpour had set in. Yet in the final hubbub of preparation, Harriet noticed that guests were steadily arriving, in cars, afoot, by team: families of the girls, boy friends, girl friends. Dashing into Jaynes Hall after a hasty inspection of the kitchen, Harriet found it buzzing with talk and laughter.

Most of the girls were excitedly greeting friends and relatives. Harriet's heart dropped as she looked round the clustering groups. How could she expect any friend or even acquaintance? Granny couldn't make the trip, and there was no one else unless ——

From a group of boys and girls a long, slim figure detached itself and approached her hesitantly, hands clasped before it, lips slowly parting over white teeth.

'Why — Richie Corwin!' she cried. They shook hands, and Harriet found that her heart had sprung up a notch and was beating a little fast, but happily, where it belonged.

'It sho' looks right pretty,' Richard said, standing beside her.

It did. Harriet had stretched wires lengthwise of the hall and hung them with streamers of silver moss, while a few feet from the side wall an entire moss curtain had been devised, with the moon glowing through it. Johnnie had thought of having that moon rise realistically by means of a pulley; but it had balked so badly when they rehearsed it, and tangled up its electric wiring so completely, that they had had to let time stand still. — 'Though I'll bet Ella had something to do with the mixup!' Harriet declared in private. — Across the end walls the booths had been built and draped gaily with bunting and crepe paper. The Landers girls, in costumes quaint or grotesque, circulated among the guests, adding to the pictorial effect.

Harriet's cheeks burned with irritation as she located Roseanne Gibbs. Catch Roseanne co-operating with a costume when she had a gorgeous new formal of gold-metal cloth! For a moment Harriet wished she had worn her chiffon; but, after all, the Harriet Tubman dress was becoming; and she had felt justified in using a little more rouge and lipstick than every day. — Nobody was co-operating very well, except the ironic Johnnie and Doxy and Countess and Hannah. The others dragged on the program like so many weights.

But — 'It sho' looks *awful* pretty,' Richard repeated,

and he was smiling shyly at her. 'I couldn' dress up,' he added regretfully, tucking his chin down to inspect his shiny, well-brushed suit.

'You look — grand!' Harriet assured him. She was thinking, 'every inch a man.' Richard was every inch a man, even if he was still only a boy.

She consulted her wrist watch. She'd lost track of time in the pressure of all the things she must do. That scavenger hunt — Looking at the older people who were gathering, she wondered feverishly whether it was going to be so easy to make them understand it. 'Why, we've got to start right now!' she exclaimed, turning toward Countess. 'Where can Miss Bates be?'

Miss Bates was not there. Miss Francis was not at the door, greeting guests. While their eyes searched for her, she came in with her quick, nervous step, and approached them. 'Harriet,' she said, 'Miss Bates is running a temperature of a hundred and one. With her health as it is, we can't let her take part tonight.'

'Lawzy!' Countess mourned. 'You reckon Roseanne Gibbs can play those pieces?'

'I can't wait to find out,' Harriet said abstractedly. She craned her neck to pick Deena May out of the crowd and beckoned her. Deena May came somewhat sulkily. — 'Deena May' — Harriet spoke in a rapid undertone — 'will you tell Ella that she and Hannah will have to help swing the singing games? And if I have to fake a lot of tunes I don't know, I don't want to worry over the scavenger hunt ——'

'You mean String Them Beans and such? — But who looks after the scag — the scagenver hunt?' Countess asked.

'It's out. There isn't going to be any,' Harriet said flatly. — Countess smiled and Deena May grinned.

Harriet lifted the whistle to her lips and cut short the

talk and laughter. 'Friends of Landers,' she said, her mouth suddenly dry, 'I'm speaking in place of Willie Lou Snyder, the president of the Senior Class. She is really in charge tonight, though illness keeps her away. She had planned the program, and we have made few changes in it.

'We are glad the rain did not keep you away, and we hope you'll enjoy the evening. In order to set the ball rolling, we will all join in the Grand March. Landers girls will pass twice round the hall so that the visitors may see the costumes and vote on the best one. Then they will lead the way across the campus to the kitchen — double-quick if it's still raining — and our guests will follow. We want you to see what the Home Economics Department has done to make the kitchen pleasanter for Miss Mitty and the girls.'

She turned, trembling from nervousness, and sat down at the piano. As soon as she spread her slim hands in a crashing chord, her nervousness vanished. Here she was quite at home.

Richard stood beside her, diffidently, watching the music with intent eyes and turning the page when the time came. She flashed a pleased glance at him: it was nice that he could read music; it was nice to have him there.

Over her shoulder she could now and then see the girls marching in couples, giggling and glancing at the audience. Johnnie was Toussaint, the famous Haitian general. She had made velvet kneebreeches out of an old skirt. Long white stockings and silver-paper shoe-buckles and lace ruffles at neck and wrists blotted out the modernness of the Norfolk jacket. She wore a cotton wig tied back with black ribbon, and a cocked hat with a feather. On her arm hung Mossie, in hoop skirt and poke bonnet.

Dresses of ten years ago, twenty, thirty, fifty, had been taken from the stores in the attic, and astonishing accessories added to them. There were a George and a Martha Washington with cotton wigs much like Toussaint's. Ella wore a rakish silk hat and a Prince Albert coat with long, sleek broadcloth skirts. The little Randalls were in sunbonnets and checked aprons.

Harriet played them out of the hall, the guests crowding after them; played till the last one was out, and then brought up the rear, with Richard. The marchers broke rank and dashed across the intervening space to the kitchen, which gleamed bright and welcoming in the rain. Richard had only time to say, 'Harriet, yo' Granny got good right to be proud of such a grand!' before they were standing in the door with Miss Francis and Miss Joan, surveying the scene.

'I do wish we could have painted the ceiling,' Miss Joan sighed.

'I wish we could have done better lettering on those cans,' added Harriet.

There was small criticism from the crowd, which had formed in double line again and was marching round and round and out into the hall and through the dining-room and back again, to the vigorous tap-tap taptaptapping of the Prince Alberted Ella. When they were not looking at each other they were admiring the racks of dishtowels spick and span and smartly marked; or the smoothly gleaming Chinese red enamel on cupboards, stools, and tables; or the ranks of containers, painted and lettered; or the clean butter-yellow of the walls.

Harriet pointed out to Richard the small rectangle, dimly discernible, which marked her disaster; and Ella heard and paused in her poker-tapping long enough to shout: 'Ought to seen 'm! Come down like Humpty Dumpty!'

'You got the message about the games?' Harriet asked.

Ella nodded brusquely. 'Can you play 'm?'

'Not very well, but I'll do the best I can.'

'Reckon it'll do,' Ella muttered.

Harriet didn't point out the lard can, big as a barrel, which Hannah had so painstakingly lettered. With one swift movement, instead, Harriet shoved and turned it until almost all its vivid lettering was hidden. Why hadn't someone noticed in time that dear Hannah had spelled out in Chinese red: 'S – H – U – G – A – R'?

When the improvements had been thoroughly inspected, Hannah started a song in which everyone joined, and those who wanted refreshments were served lemonade by a clown and sugared doughnuts by a Dutch girl with a face like an ebony cherub's (Phyllodoxia), and clinked their nickels into a bright tin dishpan held by a languid lady in the long, tight skirt and high collar of 1912.

Back at Jaynes Hall again, the program went on, and the booths were opened for business. Boys bought pop and candy and grunnets for themselves and the girls, and carried paper bags to the middle-aged and old people who could not be coaxed to leave their seats. Boys bought bait at the fish pond and dangled hook and line over the curtained corner, drawing it up with roars of laughter over the baby dolls or strings of beads that they had caught. They ventured awkwardly into the tea-room and sat with knees pressed together and balanced a plate and a cup and a wafer. From below in Countess's Chamber of Horrors sounded squeals and shrill laughter and deep guffaws to indicate the success of phosphorescent ghosts with wet rubber gloves to shake hands with, and diets of worms and all the other nonsense that became so gruesome in deep darkness with cobwebs creeping across visitors' faces.

Harriet did not have time to be 'treated' much, and she thought perhaps Richard was glad: he had probably a lean purse. She drank a root beer with him, and he bought her a bag of grunnets and a bag of candy and insisted on baiting her hook at the fish pond. There was much giggling behind the curtain when she dangled the line, and, when she jerked it up, a ten-cent-store diamond glittered on the hook. She could feel the girls watching her to see what she would do; and Richard, his lips laughing but his eyes anxious.

Harriet laughed, too, and slipped the ring on her right hand.

Presently she blew the whistle once more and announced that the judges had awarded the costume prizes to Johnnie and Mossie: a handkerchief and a blue necklace. Then she called the crowd into a game of Steal Miss Liza.

Harriet got along fairly well with the accompaniment. Richie hummed the airs for her, and that helped; but the players did not need much accompaniment. Old and young they joined in the gay old dancing, singing games:

> 'Dat ol' man ain't got no wife,
> Li'l Liza Jane.
> Cain' git one to save he's life,
> Li'l Liza Jane.
> Now won' you steal Sis' Liza,
> Li'l Liza Jane?'

Cotton wigs were mussed now, and cocked on one side; ancient dresses had suffered from having their trains stepped on; but no one was ready to stop.

> 'Git about, Cindy, Cindy.
> My peach tree's all in bloom;
> My true love gwine to marry soon;
> Git about, Cindy, Cindy!'

The evening had sped by. The booths were empty and ragged. It was time for the final Grand March. The final Grand March was marched. . . .

'Gosh, how you sing *and* play,' said Toussaint, as the last of the visitors loitered out past Miss Francis. 'And you certainly showed good judgment, letting the scavenger hunt go — even if it did mean a lot of time wasted getting ready for it. But, Harriet, have you annexed you a man? What's that Jimmie of yours going to say?'

Harriet looked startled. 'Well — Jimmie's in Minneapolis, Richard's here. But, anyway, — well, don't be silly.'

She had very nearly said, 'Can you imagine me thinking seriously of a shabby island boy who can't even use proper English?'

She could not say it: she was surprised by the warm thrill of loyalty that would not let her belittle him.

He was only a poverty-stricken and ill-educated islander. Jimmie was the son of one of the most successful Negro physicians in Minneapolis, and booked straight through for the university and medical training himself. Jimmie was a letter man, and wore his school sweater with dash. He was fun, too. Yet these few weeks had made his face fade from her mind surprisingly. She had to get out his picture to remember how he looked.

XIII

'Dose of Landers!'

THE first of the year's big games was with the Booker girls, and was to be played at Booker during Farmers' Fair, the last Saturday in November. From the day Willie Lou was taken ill, the Booker game was the chief topic of conversation: the Booker game and, first, whether Willie Lou could possibly recover soon enough to captain it; the Booker game and, next, whether Landers could possibly win it under a substitute captain; the Booker game and, finally, who that substitute captain should be.

There were two logical candidates, Harriet and Ella. Harriet ended the discussion. 'Don't be silly,' she said flatly. 'Ella's been on this team four years and I've been on four weeks. She knows your tricks and your manners. There's only one answer.'

The last Saturday in November dawned bright and beautiful. The persistent languorous warmth had sharpened at last with autumn, though the hardier flowers still bloomed — Klondike cosmos, orange-yellow; marigolds; opopanax in fluffy yellow balls; sapphire-blue spider lilies. The broomstraw was feathery with seed; and enough trees had lost their leaves to make the forest floors lovely.

The Landers truck jolted with shouts and singing over

the causeway to St. Catherine Island. At Booker the girls announced themselves with a challenging yell:

'Going to give Booker yellow janders!
How we do it? Dose of Landers!'

Miss Joan reached up and patted Harriet's hand as the girl leaned against the slatted side of the truck.

'You look happy,' she said, rather wistfully, 'you one little, two little, three little Injuns!' — and she pointed at Johnnie and Mossie, crowded up against the slats with Harriet.

Harriet thought fleetingly that the teacher herself did not look so happy these days. The girls were not seeing so much of her. They had less leisure than earlier in the term; and, besides, Miss Joan hadn't been asking them to walk and ride with her as she had formerly done.

'This school is something else again,' Miss Joan said, and they all looked around them while they waited for the truck to empty out.

The buildings stood in the perpetual twilight of an old oak forest dripping with gray moss. Today people from this island and others trooped through the dimness. Boys and girls were gathered everywhere, and when the Landers truck had driven through the gate and burst into sound, the Booker students surged forward to meet them.

Harriet looked into the throng. Smiling that bashful, wary smile of his, but with more assurance because today he was a host, Richard appeared before her as if he had shot up out of the shadowy ground, in that shadowy place that wraiths might well love.

'Mighty pleased to see you-all,' he said, pulling his foot in his old-fashioned bow.

'Mighty glad to be here!' she answered. 'Girls, you met Richard the other night. Granny's neighbor.'

The three girls jumped down from the truck and they

walked together toward the administration building, where were most of the exhibits. Richard paced slowly, hands clasped before him, eyes smiling down at Harriet.

The hall was a wild medley of sound and color and odor. The people swarmed in streams and cross-currents, crying out and cackling with laughter. Small, dark children scurried at their mothers' skirts or stood with brown legs stoutly set and stared. Exhibits were of all imaginable sorts. There were intricate quilts — Star of Bethlehem, Statehouse Steps; dresses made by girl students; canned fruit and vegetables; jelly; fine cotton bolls, full heads of rice, enormously long okra pods. A forlorn bantam rooster, some child's pet, thrust a ruffled head through the bars of its box and crowed belligerently. A calf bawled for its mother.

Harriet stopped before a table of baskets, jerking the other three to a halt with her. 'What a strange kind!' she cried.

'Yes, m'm,' Richard said, 'exackly the kind they make in Africa. Palmetto and reeds.'

She touched a beautifully shaped wood basket for the hearth, and a big, simply curved waste basket. 'They're somehow awfully lovely. Can you make them, Richard?'

'Sho' nuff! And we boys built thisyere model house in the carpenter shop.' He directed her attention to a miniature cottage outside the window. 'It taken — took — first prize in the State Housin' Contest. You-all like to see it, Harriet? — And the other young ladies?'

'If you'll excuse us, we'd like to look at the quilts instead,' Johnnie replied with excessive politeness. Mossie began an indignant protest, but Johnnie, eyes shining with amusement, dragged her away.

Richard piloted Harriet through the medley and out to the tiny house, whose roof ridge was only a few inches higher than his head. Other people were peering through

'I WANT TO MAKE SOMETHIN' OF MYSELF. I WANT TO
GET AWAY WHERE THINGS ARE DIFF'ENT'

the windows, and so did they. Four rooms the cottage had, and simple furnishings.

'Us boys made the house and the chairs and tables and bed. Girls made the curtains and rugs and paint' the walls — but they didn' fall into no bread,' he teased. 'It took first prize,' he repeated.

He gazed through those windows with the pride of achievement. Such a humble little sitting-room; such a plain little bedroom; such a primitive little kitchen; and a cubbyhole with a high window and a tin washtub and a wash basin and pitcher.

'Da's whe' dey takes dey bafs!' squealed an excited small girl whose nose was flattened against the pane at the level of Harriet's elbow. 'A hull room jes' fuh take bafs! Mah-own sis tell me.'

'If all my people could have 'm nice comf'terble homes like that,' Richie yearned.

He showed her the barns, with the beginnings of a thoroughbred herd. He showed her the rice-thresher — an experiment that had not worked out so well as expected. 'Folks go on lickin' their rice out with a stick like they've always done.'

He showed her, with vast pride, the library.

'I've been readin' all I could,' he said. 'Of late I've been readin' a sight. Reckon you-all know why.'

'You're going to college after you're through here; that's why!'

'Well — first off I want to talk better, so I don' feel so funny talkin' to you-all. You see any diff'ence, Harriet?'

'Richie, I really do.'

'An' nex', like y'all say, I want to make somethin' of myself. I want to get away where things are diff'ent.'

They were back among the exhibits now, weaving this way and that, and so interested in their own conversation that they constantly bumped into other people.

'I should think you would want to get away!' Harriet responded vehemently. Her eyes frowned at the humanity that surged around her. White headkerchiefs, sometimes topped with disreputable hats, round, black heads, rags, rags, rags; a rank smell of tobacco, though pipes were hidden here; a gabble of talk almost unintelligible.

Joan Senter had been almost lifted from her feet and carried along by the human tide. She was washed up against Harriet, and her breathless laughter was sobered by Harriet's somber face.

'Don't take it so hard!' she said swiftly. She drew Harriet, and Richard with her, into a cove behind a rack of dresses. 'Harriet, remember it's like this with any part of *any* race that has no education and no higher contacts. Weren't you ever down in the slums of a big city? Wouldn't you a lot rather have the island people's life and chance? And what about our white mountaineers?'

Harriet smiled at her. Miss Joan understood how stifled she was feeling, how weighed down by the poverty and backwardness of a great mass of her people. She pressed the teacher's arm warmly, and the three stood a while almost silent.

But it was almost the hour for the game, with no more time for idle pain or pleasure. Reluctantly Harriet threaded her way through the exhibit hall to the corridor where she was to meet her team-mates. At the corridor door Richard said, 'I'll be shoutin' for you! And, Harriet, yo're comin' over to Gentlemen's to spend Christmas with yo' Granny?'

She nodded emphatically, tossing her hand in friendly promise, and slid into the crowd of girls. She hoped she'd have a chance to throw some of those showy baskets of hers. She always wanted to play a good game, but today the desire was sharpened. She wanted to help Landers overcome the handicap of Willie Lou's absence and win the trophy for keeps. And she wanted to show Richard!

The teams were jigging up and down and shouting as all teams do, so that it seemed impossible that order should ever be wound out of the tangled skein of noise. Parents and grandparents and brothers and sisters and uncles and aunts and cousins had filled every available seat and wedged themselves into all the standing space and were hailing each other gaily. The Landers girls pranced in a file below their basket, one after another tossing the ball up and in or up and out, according to their ability.

The shrill whistle cut through the clamor and brought the centers leaping with stretched finger tips for the ball. A small and solemn boy with a crooked foot pulled himself up on a stool before the scoreboard, chalk importantly ready. The game was on.

Harriet played well and fast. Tall and long-limbed and muscular, she seemed able to shoot straight up into the air, her arms stretching elastically toward the ceiling. In the first quarter she soared upward and intercepted a Booker ball as it flew toward its basket. She captured it, dribbled it across the floor till she could pass it to Hannah, who passed it to Ella, who made a basket.

The teams were well matched. Ella and Harriet were better forwards than Booker's, but Booker had the better defence. Her guards stuck like shadows, sidling, leaping, seldom betrayed into even an accidental foul.

There was the swift patter of soft shoes on the wooden floor, like the beginning of a rain, punctuated with shouts and shrieks from the players and applause from the audience. These onlookers could howl and stamp, even if they were hazy as to the details of the game. They could scream with laughter, too, when the ball pelted into their ranks, sending them bending and scattering out of the way. And then the whistle sounded the end of the half, and the small scorekeeper rolled his eyes solemnly toward a referee for confirmation and ground the chalk against the board in staggering white numerals: Booker, 13; Landers, 12. Then the gymnasium roared like the sea.

Harriet had early located Richard. She had flashed a glance his way after her first noticeably good play and had seen him yell and wave a long hand, his face lighted with laughter; had seen his Booker companions struggle to silence him, laughing also. — It was much more fun to win glory when someone was cheering especially for you! Now in the last half she wished with every beat of her pounding heart to make a score, a spectacular basket, for her own glory and for Landers.

Back and forth raced the ball, accompanied by the patter and rush of feet: up to one end, down to the other, too swiftly for accurate baskets. Mossie, doubling and running and making a long slide as if on ice, grabbed the ball beneath Booker's basket and dribbled it rapidly up the floor. Mossie almost never fouled in her dribbling: she seemed to dance with the bounce of the ball: step-bounce, step-bounce, quick and true.

Ella roared a 'Hy-ah!' that they had answered in a dozen practice games, and Mossie, feinting to pass the ball to the left, shot it, lightning quick, to the right and Ella. Harriet, just left of the center, poised unguarded, and the ball smacked into her hands. She swung around, gauged direction and distance for a long, tense moment, and then hurled the ball toward the basket. It hovered — it dropped — and the room rocked with cheers and groans. The solemn little boy, who had been staring at the game over his shoulder, turned back and erased the figures and slowly traced: for Booker, 13; for Landers, 14.

Again ball and team eddied to and fro. Playing was again too fast and excited for scoring, but Ella plunged against a Booker girl, and in the resulting penalty Booker made a free throw and tied the score.

Time was jumping past. Again Mossie had the ball, slid between opposing guards, step-bounce, step-bounce. Again she passed it to Harriet, well toward the center. Again Harriet, catching it, made swift calculation.

It was her chance for one more spectacular throw, and Landers' chance for victory. If she missed, the game would be a tie, or worse.

And almost under the basket, for an instant unguarded again, Ella waited tiptoe.

Swift and straight the ball flew toward Ella's hands. With the speed of light it rose from those hands, up, up above the basket, where it arched and fell gracefully into place. The whistle shrilled. The game was over.

The solemn boy, his very knickerbockers creeping dejectedly toward his toes, plaintively marked the final score: 16 to 14 for Landers.

High over the heads of the crowd Richard waved to Harriet. Ella said grudgingly, 'You sho' knows teamwork, Hat!' — The other Landers girls grabbed their forwards and hoisted them on their shoulders, where they rode, tilting, clutching, laughing, out to the truck. Joan Senter made a megaphone of her hands and shouted, 'Six little — hundred little Injuns!'

It was true: Harriet and Johnnie and Mossie no longer stood alone against Landers.

But next morning the depression which had beset Harriet in the exhibit hall engulfed her again. She was writing one of the three weekly letters permitted students: writing to Mrs. Trindle.

'Sometimes I feel as if I can't stand another day of this. Some things about it I'm getting to love, but others — ! Well, I suppose you've felt it yourself, like a big weight dragging you back — our people. "My people," Richard

Corwin would say. But it's too awful to feel that these thousands without hope *are* my people. And that, in a way, we can't any of us rise until they are all lifted up. It's like being crushed under a burden too heavy to bear.'

XIV

Miss Bates

DECEMBER's three weeks of school had more than they could hold.

The classes were vying with each other in money-making projects. The cooking teacher let the Seniors make benny candy. Roseanne Gibbs brought out a box of the famous 'peach leather,' from Charleston. The rolls of it, like tiny orange-brown diplomas, had to be sold at a nickel apiece. The Juniors bought quantities of grunnets and roasted them and sold them, hot and good, for five cents a bag.

Peanut shells were everywhere, tumbling out of desks and littering grass and rolling from under beds. The art teacher had all her classes make posters:

KEEP LANDERS CLEAN!
Put the nuts into your mouths
and the shells into the wastebaskets!

Girls were chinking in the time with the making of Christmas gifts: needle and thread, pen and ink, paste, knitting needles, crochet hooks, were forever being thrust under pillows or into pockets or sat on when an intended recipient suddenly appeared. Harriet had finished an elaborate trousseau for her doll, and spent September on a present for Granny. She looked long at clever apron patterns and pretty nightgowns; but her sense of humor pictured Granny's dark dignity in them, and she laughed and cut long-sleeved, high-necked outing nightgowns, with conventional round collars. She sent boxes of peach leather and benny candy to her three best friends in Minneapolis; to the Trindles, besides more conventional gifts, sprays of holly and mistletoe and Spanish moss.

The Christmas tree, erected in the middle of Landers dining-hall at the final dinner before the holidays, was a gay affair. Everyone was well remembered. Harriet found on the tree a bunch of sugar cane from Mossie, a snapshot of Washington Hall, framed in seashells, from Hannah, a handkerchief from Willie Lou, a book from Johnnie, a carefully embroidered collar from Phyllodoxia. She had received several packages from Minneapolis — from the Trindles a beautifully knitted rust-colored dress which Mrs. Trindle must have had to hurry to finish.

Joan Senter stealthily slipped small parcels to Harriet and Johnnie. 'You know I got the dickens from the faculty,' she explained, with a puckered grin above her sober little double chin. 'That was for singling out favorite companions among the students. I suppose they're right. I'm not so grown-up and sensible as I thought I was. — But that's why I've seemed to be so busy lately.'

'Mother told me,' Johnnie said gravely. 'But she said not to repeat it. She said you were a dear, Miss Joan. She said the only thing wrong with you was youth, and she hoped you wouldn't be in any hurry to get over that.'

'Good gracious!' Harriet exploded. 'You don't have as much social life as we do, even.'

'Oh, well!' — the young teacher achieved a fairly

nonchalant manner — 'it won't be for long. They haven't any place for me in Landers after this semester, even if I wanted to stay. And my old school has offered me the crafts classes. It will be a lovely job, like a bed of roses, comparatively speaking.'

The climax of the campus celebration was the musical program that night. The girls, in white dresses or dresses as nearly white as they possessed, wound their way across the campus at first dark, each carrying a candle thrust through a cardboard disk, and sang. They sang the Christmas carols, and Harriet led. They sang the spirituals, and Hannah led. 'Ain' gwine study war no more...' — 'Oh, my lovin' sister, when the world's on fire...' How they loved to sing them! How Harriet thrilled to hear them, especially like this, looking back on the long misty line curving beneath the black trees, taper flames glimmering ——

In the big living-rooms at Sarah B., a fire burned in the fireplace and the candles were set everywhere, in decorative holders made by Miss Joan's classes from tin salvaged from the dump heap. Miss Francis read the Christmas story: 'And there were in the same country shepherds, keeping watch by night over their flocks...'

So quiet the rooms. So sweet and holy all the still-burning flames.

Harriet played. After her ability had been betrayed by the Carnival, it was a foregone conclusion that she should play. She played another carol, with the whole room crooning it. She played 'Humoresque,' 'Souvenir,' — proved popular by thousands of radios. And then she played Chopin's 'Prelude' in F, on which she had been working, together with Beethoven's 'Moonlight Sonata,' in those early morning practice hours all fall.

She did not know quite why she played it: perhaps it was a way of saying to Miss Bates, 'You see? I've gone pretty far to be expected to take lessons of a little music teacher who teaches beginners only.'

She played well. Even the girls, stirring uneasily, looked at her with wide eyes in the glimmer.

There was more singing, and Roseanne Gibbs rendered, not too badly, 'To a Wild Rose.' Miss Bates followed Roseanne at the piano. She also played popular classics: 'Herd Girl's Dream,' and 'Traümerei.' Then she paused for a long moment and played the 'Moonlight Sonata.'

Harriet listened in growing amazement. She had known that Miss Bates played correctly and with good touch, but until tonight she had heard her do nothing but accompaniments. The sonata, with its range of technique, its range of emotion, was done as she had never heard it. To a group of a hundred schoolgirls on a sea island of South Carolina ——

After most of the other girls had gone, Harriet waited, while the teachers went about putting out a hundred candles that were guttering down to inch-high mounds of white. When she approached Miss Bates, Miss Bates turned to her with a smile that was tender as well as amused.

'Your "Prelude" was beautifully done,' she said. 'I've heard you many mornings when I've gone down through the drying-yard to watch the sun rise out of the bay — The sun comes up as big and red and gorgeous when you see it from the drying-yard as anywhere else ——'

'Then it was really you I heard, one night in the fall, playing Bach. I thought the wind carried it from one of those mansions in Bosquet. Or that it was a fairy ——'

'I practise from ten to twelve, or thereabouts. And you from five to seven. And so we've kept apart, with the whole day between us.'

Harriet stood with compressed lips and downcast eyes. She had felt superior to this 'little music teacher.' And

now, what could she say? She couldn't say, 'Oh, Miss
Bates, you play so beautiful!' as the girls had done. She
couldn't even echo Miss Francis: 'It was a privilege to
listen.' Her feeling was too big for any expression she
could give it.

She lifted troubled eyes. '*Why?*' she stammered.

'Why?'

'Why — *here?*'

Miss Bates sat down on one of the hard settles and
motioned Harriet to sit beside her. Half consciously
Harriet noticed again the grace of the sitting, in one long
flowing movement; the grace of her beckoning hand.

'It's too long a story,' the teacher said. 'My father was
a musician, too, and dreamed great things for me. And
gave his life' — she laid a significant hand on her breast
— 'to make them come true. Expensive teachers —
schools ——'

'They did come true?'

'Yes, they did come true. For such a little while. And
then — you know how susceptible our race has been to
tuberculosis — then long months in a mountain sani-
tarium. And then this. — And I've loved it very much.'

'Teaching Ella Hooper to play "Lightly Row"?'
Harriet demanded fiercely.

Miss Bates chuckled. 'Giving them all the music they
can hold, in every way possible. That's going to make a
difference to a hundred schoolhouses in the woods and
fields; to a hundred hundred homes. — And here I am,
living in all this beauty instead of going out quickly —
like that candle — in another concert season or two.
That's what the doctors said: a season or two of public
life, gay and glamorous, and that would be all. Now I'm
giving something. And having Beethoven, just the same.
And going to Charleston every week, so that life doesn't
become too — tight.

'That's all, my dear. But mostly — I hate to sound priggish, but it's true — mostly happiness is *giving* something.'

Miss Bates had risen, with that sweet fluid motion, but Harriet sat dumbly looking up at her.

'Magdalen Bates!' she said, as one who speaks out of a dream. 'Mother used to speak of you. — And *I* can have lessons of — Magdalen Bates.'

'The pianos aren't so good,' said Magdalen Bates, 'but it might be worth two dollars a month.'

XV

'Go Tell It on de Mountains'

HALF of Christmas belonged to Landers. The other half began when Harriet again took boat for Gentlemen's Island, the day before Christmas. Huddled in her warmest coat she sat as before on the open deck, where now the wind blew keen.

It seemed perfectly natural for Richard to meet her at the dock and carry her suitcases for her. This time the air had a crispness that made the walk a delight. And immediately upon landing Harriet tasted Christmas. People were crowding round the one little store down near the shore — the store where R. Corwin had got the stale stationery — buying and shouting and laughing and shooting firecrackers. The cabins that sunned themselves along the road had their front doors and window shutters gleaming white, and no one was lounging on the porches.

'Because it's Christmas Eve,' Richard explained. 'Ever we whitewash with oystershell lime and clean up and trim up nice for Christmas.'

'I hope Granny has a big apron, so I can get right to work helping her!' Harriet cried.

143

'No need to spoil yo' nice hands,' he said, smiling his big, kind smile. 'Lily and Granny and me, we've made it pretty a'ready.'

They crunched through a short cut, where the keen smell of fallen leaves rose around them. And there stood the cabin. Granny's marigolds still bloomed bravely, and late chrysanthemums were wine and snow. And never were door and shutters more glisteningly white than Granny's.

Harriet had only an instant to admire them before Granny answered the creak of the gate and came hurrying across the porch, her headkerchief and apron as dazzling as the whitewash, her gold hoop earrings bobbing, her face radiant. Lily, scrubbed and shining, too, ducked under Granny's arm and dashed at them, grabbing the suitcases and staggering into the house with them, grinning back over her shoulder.

Harriet went straight into Granny's outstretched arms.

'But come in, come in, Richie, 'n' res' yo' hat an' coat!' Granny remembered to urge, wiping away the tears with a starchy apron corner. 'Ain' got no manners, nohow.'

The cabin took them in with almost the same warmth and welcome as Granny. Lily, when she had deposited the suitcases and bustled away with Harriet's hat and coat and gloves, went jigging around scrutinizing Harriet from all angles and watching to see if she noticed with proper appreciation the dressing up of the room.

All the walls and the ceiling and the insides of doors and shutters had been papered with fresh newspapers, so that no sharp breezes could come through anywhere except at the cracks in the floor, where the freshly washed rag rugs lifted a little. Door and window curtains were snow white.

'Lily cut the trimmin's for the mantel,' Richard

murmured under his breath, nodding toward the cut-out newspaper.

Lily grinned whitely when Harriet exclaimed over those scallops, and rolled her eyes toward the 'big girl' from the tin can of chrysanthemums which she was regarding with sudden absorption.

'The flowers likewise,' Richard explained, and Harriet praised them to the child's satisfaction.

Beneath Lily's newspaper edging the fire snapped and sparkled and made the room alive. From the kitchen came mingled food odors of Christmas: grapy, fruity smells; smells of spice and molasses and fresh bread. Harriet's eyes filled with tears. She had not believed that Christmas could ever make her so happy again.

Proud to do the honors, Lily led her into the kitchen and showed her the bottles of colored juices and the glasses of jelly on the shelves; the strings of red peppers hanging from the walls.

'Traded me some hens fuh fresh hog-meat,' Granny said happily.

And — 'Don' e smell good?' demanded Lily, lifting the lid of a kettle and licking her lips with exaggerated delight.

It did smell good: rice, Harriet could see, bubbling deliciously with tidbits of meat and seasonings of scarlet pepper.

'But us gots chicken fuh Christmas,' Lily whispered loudly. 'And — Granny, kin I show 'm de fruit-cake?'

She hopped and skipped to the cupboard and lugged out a crock, hugging it in skinny arms. 'Smell 'm!' she commanded.

'Scuppernong wine on de crus',' said Granny, as if that explained the peculiarly delicate fragrance. 'Made tereckly after Thanksgiving.'

Harriet stood in the back door, flung open to the

December sunshine. The fallen fig tree had been cleared away and the henhouse rebuilt.

'And who ever chopped all that wood?' Harriet asked.

'E did!' Lily crowed, sighting impishly along her finger at Richard. 'E chop de wood and e white de do's and e fetch de scup'nongs and de hick'ry nuts and de wil' crabapples.'

'Care if I walk over to the meetin'-house with you-all tonight?' Richard asked hastily.

Harriet looked questioningly at Granny. 'Do we go to the meeting-house?' she asked.

Granny nodded as she stirred the savory rice. 'Sho' we does. It Chris'mas Eve. Please' to have y'all, Richie.'

Richard went home, and Lily watched with wide eyes and buttoned-up mouth as Harriet unpacked her suitcases. Harriet showed her the contents of some of the packages, with the result that Lily went dancing wildly around the cabin, making eyes at Granny and exploding with the laughter that she tried to hold in. Other packages Harriet sneaked carefully on the tiptop of the old wardrobe; yet not so carefully that Lily should not see them being hidden and go bouncing with a vehement joy that shook the cabin. Guessing but not knowing — that was a big part of a little girl's fun.

Supper was early. Granny filled and refilled the 'chillen's' plates and watched their zest with deep-eyed content. And as soon as the hens were shut up and the dishes washed and the fires carefully banked and clothes and hair tidied, the bong-bong-bong of a cowbell sounded from afar. Lily pranced, where she stood, like a jumping-jack whose string has been jerked.

'It de meetin'-house! It de meetin'-house!' she squealed, and dived for her red sweater on its nail behind the door. At the same moment Richard tapped and came in.

'Isn't there any way of locking up?' Harriet inquired,

when they were all ready to go. Her tissue-wrapped Christmas gifts were small enough, but she was uneasy at the thought of leaving them in an open house.

'Lockin' up?' — Granny chuckled richly — 'Don' got to lock no do's on Gentlemen's, honey!'

Mule teams, horse teams, ox-carts, and two or three rusty cars were massed around Jericho Church. It was packed with dark humanity. Its whitewashed walls were hidden by the people, and the dim kerosene lamps high along the side walls illumined the sharp glitter of teeth and eyes in the duskiness.

Harriet felt a million miles away from last Christmas Eve. Then a group of their young people had been carried around the Twin Cities in automobiles, to see the outdoor lighting and to sing carols in the crisp, snowy darkness. — 'The first Noël the angels did say!' How she had loved those archaic words, lifted down from the Middle Ages! How she had loved the revival of the old custom!

Yet there was something artificial about that revival. There was nothing artificial about this celebration. It was old custom coming down unbroken from the past.

The Christmas story was read from the Bible, while old voices and young murmured praise. Old hymns were sung, lined out by the leader because there were no hymnals, and many, to be sure, who could not read.

People prayed and gave testimony, with everyone else joining, as at that first church service Harriet had attended. Children sprawled over their mothers' laps and slept, or bobbed their heads against parental shoulders. Richard shyly directed Harriet's attention to a dark Madonna across the church from them, a delicious brown three-year-old sleeping in her arms, his dimpled knees bare. A boy of sixteen or so, beside them, grinned knowingly at Richard and let his eyes move on to Harriet. 'My-own folks,' Richard said. 'Mom wants you and

Granny should have dinner with us whilst yo' here.'
Harriet found her eyes irresistibly drawn to Mrs. Corwin
and Aaron and Baby Washington. The eyes played a
game across the crowded room all night.

Before the evening was far spent, Lily's head had
bobbed down on Granny's lap. Harriet felt her own eyes
drooping, her head nodding, even in all the rise and fall of
sound about her. Richard nudged her gently and she
came awake with a start, hoping she had not had her
mouth open. She looked at the boy beside her, in acute
embarrassment, and he smiled back gently, humorously.
The kindest person, Richard!

'It mos' midnight,' he whispered. 'I knowed — knew —
you'd want to listen for cock-crow.'

A hush held the congregation, and far off in the still
dark sounded the faint, high paean of a cock: another;
another.

Then indeed did the voice of petition change to the
voice of praise and joy. The frail building shook with
hallelujahs and the rhythmic patting of feet. Spiritual
after spiritual was led off and joined by the congregation.

Lily sat up with a jerk, muttering hoarsely: 'Granny, is
our cow kneelin' down fuh sho'? An' Nicky, too?'

'So they says, honey, so they says,' Granny answered
her softly.

Harriet looked a startled query at Richard.

'Ain' — haven' — you ever heard it?' he asked. 'All
the old folks say so: that the cows and the critters and all
the beasts, they kneel to pray at Christmas Eve, just like
humans. — Like enough it ain' so,' he added hastily, 'but
it's pretty.'

Lily dropped back to sleep. Granny's head swayed
forward till her chin rested on her white neckerchief, and
then jerked upright as she opened suspicious eyes. The

lamps smoked and grew dimmer. The air thickened. Harriet kept dozing, rocked by the vibration.

Again she wakened, finding Richard's smile upon her, hoping again that her mouth had not fallen open, feeling a rush of cool fresh air from the open doors. A thin light filtered into the church, paling the lamp flames. The voices of the people rose with fresh eagerness.

'Go tell it on de mountains, Dat Jesus Christ is a-born!'

'It's day-clean!' whispered Richard. 'The sun has come up, shoutin' the praise of the Lord.'

That cherry-red sun might have been shouting, but the tuneful clamor of the people would have drowned any sound but their own.

By the time Granny and her trio had left the throng and walked a little way, the keen air had washed away the night's stale sleepiness. Richard carried Lily pickaback, and Harriet walked arm-in-arm with Granny. Harriet thought there had never been anything so beautiful as this Christmas morning, edged with frost and animated by the early song of birds and the flash of rabbits across the road and the whirring of partridges from a thicket.

'Does us git our stockin's now?' Lily demanded, when Richard set her down on Granny's porch.

'You-all piles into bed an' has you a nap befo' breakfast,' Granny told her. 'Den you kin see has Sandy Claw been here. Don' you look yit!'

Lily staggered sleepily through the room, face set rigidly ahead but big eyes rolling sidewise toward the mantel. 'Sandy Claw ain' came! E ain' came!' she whimpered uncontrollably.

'Jes' wait twell after breakfast and see!' Granny counseled, spanking her gently toward the bed.

'Cain' sleep nohow!' Lily protested, knuckling heavy eyes as Granny pulled the dress off over her twenty braids. 'Cain' ——' The words were engulfed in a wide yawn and she rolled over into the big feather bed and was asleep.

Harriet and Granny filled the child's stocking, and while Harriet washed her face and combed her hair, she could hear Granny crackling starchily around the fire.

While Granny was cooking breakfast, Harriet filled still another stocking and hung it back in the shadows, where it would not be quickly observed. So when breakfast was ready and the shutters thrown wide to the good Christmas sun, and Lily wakened, three stockings hung in delightful distortion before that snapping fire. Little attention did the savory breakfast receive from little girl or big, though Granny urged and scolded.

A doll smiled from the top of Lily's Christmas stocking, as a doll should smile from the top of every little girl's. It was the yellow-haired doll which Harriet had dressed in sewing class. Its present costume was a pair of outing-cloth pajamas and bedroom slippers that Harriet had contrived from scraps of felt.

'E *too* pretty! Dis de clo'es de buckruh wear fo' Sunday bes', enty?' Lily asked rapturously, holding the doll at arm's length to admire her and snatching her to her breast to love her.

Harriet laughed. 'It's what "de buckruh" wear for sleepy-time. You just wait and see what else is in the stocking.'

Lily clawed out a polished apple and a poke of molasses candy, and probed among the nuts till she fished out a tissue-wrapped parcel soft to the touch. It disclosed small underclothes, nicely made to the last snap and buttonhole. Still farther down was a checked gingham dress, and below it a knitted coat and hat, socks, and slippers.

Under the stocking was a new dress for Lily herself, from Granny. And in the stocking's toe was a small box which revealed a silver ring set with a turquoise. It had been Harriet's ring, and she had remembered Mother's saying: 'A doll-baby in the top and a finger ring in the toe: that surely does make the right kind of Christmas stocking for a girl child.'

Ring on finger, Lily dressed and undressed her doll. Her hands trembled and her tongue protruded from the bud of her lips. She was dumb with joy.

'You-all ain' peek at yo' own stockin', Hayet,' Granny reminded her.

Apples. Nuts. A knitted scarf from Granny. A bottle of dreadful perfume from Lily, who woke up from her doll to beam when Harriet took it out. On the floor below the stocking, a bulky bundle: a quilt of beautiful old design, quilted with tiny stitches.

'For me?' cried Harriet.

Granny nodded, eyes moist with delight at the girl's surprise. 'E de Statehouse Steps pattern,' she said. 'Done began piecin' 'm when I got yo' letter las' summer.'

'And you haven't looked at *your* stocking, Granny!' Harriet reminded her in turn.

'Mussy me! I ain' hang no stockin' dis fifty year!' — Her eyes followed Harriet's finger, pointing to the black length in the shadows. — 'Why, honey chile, whenever did you-all —— ?'

Chuckling with embarrassment, Granny sat down in her rocker and held her aproned lap for the treasure. Lily had traded the eggs from her pet hens and bought a bottle of hair-straightener over which Granny giggled and clicked her teeth. Granny stroked her thick, fleecy nightgowns almost as delightedly as Lily stroked her doll, and examined the pink embroidery on the yoke of the blue one and the blue embroidery on the yoke of the pink one with indrawn breaths of admiration. And in the toe of Granny's stocking, too, was something small and precious in a jeweler's box: a small brooch that had been Mother's, with a chip diamond sparkling in its twist of gold. At sight of that, Granny threw a nightgown over her face and rocked to and fro, crying softly.

'What are you going to name your new doll, Lily?' asked Harriet, shy of tears.

Lily looked up solemnly: 'I name 'm Granny Hayet Queener Sheber.'

From the door Richard's laughter echoed theirs. He did not come empty-handed. He had one of the hand-woven wastebaskets for Harriet, a string of beads for Lily, and for Granny a sack of rice and a broom, hand-made from wild broom grass bound with split hickory.

Shyly Harriet handed him a parcel that had lain on the mantel, lovely in star-strewn blue wrapping paper and silver bows. Richard turned it over and over. 'E too pretty fuh spile!' he murmured, lapsing into Gullah talk. He sat with knees stiffly pressed together and awkwardly slipped off the ribbon and folded the paper, before looking at the book, 'American Cities.'

'Never did I own a book befo', cep'n' the Good Book and schoolbooks,' he said soberly.

Eyes shining with eagerness, Lily plumped Granny Hayet Queener Sheber down on the open pages of the book and followed her with all her wardrobe and waved the turquoise ring so close to Richard's eyes that he flinched involuntarily. Then she exhibited the perfume she had given Harriet and the hair-straightener that she had given Granny.

When all the presents had been inspected, Harriet looked longingly at the open window. 'Let's walk!' she proposed.

With Lily scampering around them, ahead of them, like a dog that runs three miles to its master's one, Harriet and Richard tramped around the island. Again squirrels and rabbits and quail darted through the underbrush, and fallen leaves crunched underfoot. Richard had a pocketful of peanuts and a length of white sugar cane apiece, and he showed Harriet a more satisfactory technique for chewing and sucking the oldtime Southern sweet.

'Got to get my book an' go home,' he said reluctantly, when they returned to the cabin. 'Promise' to take Mom an' li'l Washin'ton to Booker for the Mystery.'

He passed a loving hand over the book cover.

'You simply must see all those cities some day,' Harriet said eagerly.

'I'm gwine to,' he answered simply. 'Done made up my mind.'

XVI

'WE RE LUCKY!'

THE morning after Christmas Harriet was wakened by a flood of cool air and a red gleam full in her face. She snuggled down under the weight of quilts and stared sleepily. The sun was shining straight in at the window — an open window which had certainly been shuttered when she went to bed.

Granny was not beside her. She was kneeling before that window in her high-necked, long-sleeved nightgown — a patched nightgown, for she was saving the new ones. While Harriet blinked drowsily, the old woman bowed her grizzled head to the floor, once, twice, three times.

'La-la-la-la-la!' she intoned as if humming in her deep voice; and then, very simply, 'Blessed King Jesus, keep Yo' li'l chillen safe and good dis day, Amen!'

Harriet squeezed her eyes shut before Granny struggled stiffly to her feet and turned to dress. That morning obeisance was so strange!

The strangeness hovered in her mind through the hurry of washing and dressing. Richard was going to take her over to Saint Catherine's today, and when he came to milk they must make their plans.

154

We're Lucky!

While she was slipping her dress over her head she heard the boy's thumping at the back door, and when she ran out to the kitchen to say good morning the air was aromatic with warm milk.

It was a fine crisp day for an excursion. Richard's bateau was staked on the bay beach. They ran lightly across the strip of quaking sand and established themselves, and Harriet watched with eager interest as Richard set the oars in the oarlocks and pulled out with long strokes into the salt-smelling water.

'Set right still!' he warned her.

'Oh, I've been in rowboats before. We have lakes in Minnesota: pretty little ones all through Minneapolis and St. Paul and big ones with pine and white birch up through the north of the state.'

'Gwine see 'm!' he boasted, grinning at her. 'Gwine see 'm all!'

She puckered her brows. 'I — don't know whether I've ever seen anything lovelier than this, though!' She waved her arm in a comprehensive gesture.

'Shucks!' he deprecated. 'Y'all are just bein' mannersable.'

Saint Catherine's was lovely, too, in the afternoon sunshine. When Richard had tied his boat they tramped through the sweetness of it, he with his oars over his shoulder. The road that led to Booker was an even more shadowy tunnel than the Landers highway; and more ox-carts squalled past them, and more mule teams with no harness except rope reins and ropes to hold up the sapling thills.

Miss Locke's house stood in a sunny garden a stone's throw from the nearest of the school buildings. Walks made of great round stepping stones led between frosted chrysanthemums and marigolds with a few hardy blossoms, up to a deep-porched bungalow. Harriet set foot on a stone and paused. It was strangely grooved and marked.

'Millstones,' Richard answered her unspoken query.

'But I don't see ———'

'Old-style ones, somethin' like the kind in the Good Book, I reckon. Mom tells how there was a big flood back in 1911 and the island folks was in a bad fix. So the teachers at Booker say if they bring their old millstones to make Booker a walk they'll give 'em food and clo'es for 'em. You see there ain' no rocks on the whole of the island.'

Miss Locke, small, erect, blue-eyed and white-haired, met them cordially at the door. She had a welcoming hand for Richard and a questioning smile for Harriet. Richard made the introduction with simple dignity, and, seated in the quietly charming living-room, Harriet came quickly to the point.

'Miss Locke, what can be done about the island farms that are being sold for taxes? My great-grandmother's tract — it seems that it was sold years ago. Do you suppose I can get it back for her?'

Miss Locke's face shone. 'Are you one of the boys and girls who are going to work for their people here?' she asked. 'Richard is another. He's a real Booker lad, even if he has had only a few years with us. We're looking to such boys to play a big part on their own islands in a few more years. We need girls just as badly.'

Harriet shook her head. 'No, I haven't thought of staying more than this year. I mean to go back and enter the University of Minnesota. I'll be a music major, but I'm going to minor in Home Economics. — I do want to see what can be done about Granny's home, though.'

She glanced at Richard. He was twirling his cap, his face cloudy.

'Well,' Miss Locke conceded, 'there are other places to work. I suppose it's natural I see this one. There's a great deal to build on in these islands.' She smiled

abstractedly past them out of the window. 'But your
great-grandmother's home ——' She recalled herself.

'It's in that bunch of farms boughten up by Mr. Van
Buren from up No'th,' Richard explained.

She nodded. 'Oh, yes, just before the Depression. I've
looked into that. He lost practically everyting in 1929,
and he hasn't paid the taxes on those farms since he
bought them.'

'He hasn't?' Harriet's voice was eager. 'Doesn't that
mean that we could buy them back? Or would it cost too
much?'

'A hundred dollars might cover your grandmother's
tract. But after that there would be the problem again
of making it productive enough to support her and who-
ever else is dependent on her, and pay the current taxes
as she goes. Richard has it well planned. He can do it,
too; and not only that, but help all the others on the island
to do it.'

She smiled at them sparklingly and swept on.

'Richard harvested the prize crop of sweet potatoes on
his school acre this fall. Seven times the average yield for
South Carolina. You can see what such productiveness
would mean to the farmers. That's why Richard wears a
Booker sweater, like a letter man at home. — You work
Mrs. Freeman's ground too, don't you, Richard?'

'My brother and me.'

'Well, you see they can make the farms pay if they work
scientifically. Tell her how you apportion your crops,
Richard.'

Richard went on twirling his cap, while he told Harriet,
heavily, how they planted for provisions for the household
and provisions for the animals and a 'money crop' that
would give them the small amounts of cash necessary.

'But Richard's plan is much bigger than this. He's
learning to do everything that's needed on a farm, from

re-tiring a cart and making harness to breeding good stock; and as soon as he's through here and maybe had an advanced year at Hampton, the Government will put him in as instructor on his own island, to work through the rural schools there. You can't measure his value!'

'But his music?' Harriet asked.

'His music will always be an asset beyond price.' Miss Locke smiled again, expectantly, at Richard, but he was still twirling his cap.

'These *are* your plans, Richard?' Alarm sharpened her voice.

'Lessen I get me a good job up No'th — just for a while — and make money enough to send back to my people and help 'm thataway,' Richard answered.

Miss Locke's brows lifted in concern. 'I can't think you would do that,' she said in a carefully controlled voice. 'You've too much vision, Richard. Money can't help your people as you yourself can help them — help them to help themselves.' She studied him anxiously, but he would not meet her eye. 'I can't imagine where a boy or girl could invest life better than right here. There's a sounder basis here for most of our small landowners than anywhere in the North, where life is so often tawdry and sordid for them. Here you could be a sort of Moses ——'

Richard seized the name as an escape.

'Miss Locke, there's another thing Harriet wants to find out,' he said quickly. 'Somethin' about her great-great-great grandpa. Black Moses, he was called. On Tolliver Plantation.'

Miss Locke still studied him, her eyes somber with disappointment. Harriet helped him past the awkward silence.

'They say strange things about him, Miss Locke. Legends like the legends of Paul Bunyan of the Northwest, about his size and strength. But the most interesting things are about his being — well, the son of a priest some-where in Northern Africa, and reading and writing in another tongue. Yet Granny' — Harriet flushed — 'Granny can't read or write our own.'

Again Miss Locke had recalled herself courteously. 'Yes, I have heard of him. I've heard of him as a leader not unworthy of his name. He was hampered by one of the harder type of masters' — she broke off; began again — 'but whatever his origin and whatever his condition here, he was a nobleman. Any descendant of Black Moses has reason to be proud.'

Harriet's high head was higher as she shook hands in farewell; but Miss Locke was thinking less about her than about Richard. Her blue eyes rested on him ponder-ingly.

'Richard,' she said, 'your life is your own. But look at some of the boys that have gone North. Don't they seem — shoddy — compared to Sam Fripp, working on Hilton's Head for his people?'

'Reckon it depends on what's inside 'm in the first place,' Richard dissented. 'Looks like we-all ought to see somethin' beyond our own islands, m'm.'

Unaccountably, Miss Locke's face had brightened. 'I guess you're right in one thing, Richard,' she said more serenely. 'It depends on what you really *are*, inside.'

As they walked back toward the bay and the boat, Harriet's elation bubbled through a certain depression that had settled upon her. 'It does seem marvelous what you can do here! It's a — a profession. And something that seems to be building for the future, too. Isn't it stupid how we choose little things to do with our lives, when we could just as well choose big ones? — Richard!' she broke off to scold, 'why are you acting so funny about it today?'

'Shucks!' He grinned down at her. 'Y'all get me eye-sighted over seein' the world and then you scold me caze I want to see it. Cain' do nothin' about it anyway, Harriet. My lef' foot done itch for a week.'

'Your foot itches?'

'Sure sign,' he said, grinning. 'Gwine travel strange ground.'

'Who's the swanky-looking boy?' Harriet interrupted softly.

'Lawzy, if it ain' Jick Smith,' Richard answered without pleasure.

Jick Smith was sauntering out to a dilapidated gateway, smiling as he came. Richard tossed a hand in salute and hastened his steps, but Jick did not take the hint. He creaked open the gate and confronted them.

'Miss Freeman,' Richard said unwillingly, 'meet Jick Smith. He just came from up No'th.'

Jick nodded. 'Seen you before, ain' I? Don't have to ask are you from the No'th, Miss Freeman. Gwine back in a hurry, too, I bet you. So'm I. Never could stan' the sticks.'

'Oh, but I think these islands are lovely,' Harriet replied coolly. She recognized Jick. He was the boy with the round dimple in his cheek, the boy who had stuck her pink paper napkin behind his ear on the boat.

She knew his type. He was present in every group of society and in every color. There was something winning about his impudence, something fascinating about his cakewalking swing as he came to meet them, his feet cutting little flourishes, with style and precision. But he was spoiled and sure of himself. Harriet loved to take that sort down a peg. So she looked at him 'down her nose,' as Johnnie expressed it.

'We've got to hurry, Richie,' she said, 'or Granny'll be worried. Good-bye, Mr. Smith.'

Richard kept glancing at her anxiously as they ap-

'WH' Y'ALL WANTS TO KNOW, HONEY CHILE?'

proached the bateau. 'Handsome, ain't he — isn't he?' he asked.

'Who? That Jick person? Say, Richard, wasn't he one of the ones Miss Locke meant when she spoke of the fellows who had been living North?'

'Maybe so.'

'Well, I don't know Sam Fripp; but I kept putting this slick Jick up against — Black Moses,' Harriet said soberly. 'Richie, haven't you heard anything more about Black Moses?'

'Ask Granny,' he suggested, helping her into the boat. 'Ask her tonight. I fetched her some pa'tridges and she invited me to supper. I like to hear tales about Black Moses, my-own self.'

The sun was setting red when they reached the home beach and drove the boat in among the rushes. The air was so keen that Harriet snuggled her fur collar up around her ears and Richard slapped his hands together for warmth as they strode through the field and through the thicket to Granny's cabin. The opening door let out a rush of fragrant warmth. Supper was making, and by the time Richard had washed himself scrupulously and milked, the meal was ready to dish up.

The partridges were delicate morsels, and the pork chitterlings and rice supplemented them gratefully. Harriet ate until she was sure she could never eat again.

Yet after the dishes were washed and the fire was made up in the sitting-room fireplace, she was not sorry to see Granny putting grunnets to roast in the ashes.

'Granny,' she said, 'while the peanuts are roasting, won't you tell us about Black Moses?'

Granny looked at her questioningly, smoothing Lily's head with a big dark hand. 'Wh' y'all wants to know, honey chile?'

'Well — what language was it he read and wrote?

And why didn't he teach you reading and writing?
And ——'

'Ain' dat 'nough fuh start on, honey?' Granny asked,
shifting Lily to a more comfortable position on her lap.
'Why e ain' teach me? Caze e done dead befo' I done born.
Black Moses ain' so old when e dead,' Granny explained
somberly, and rocked creakingly back and forth before
she added: 'Mammy tell us stories, but I fuhgit 'm. But
I do know Ol' Mas'r beat e's darkies efn dey learn readin'
an' writin'.'

'Yet they keep telling us that most masters were kind,'
Harriet protested.

'Mebbe mos' of 'm was,' Granny agreed, stroking Lily's
head against her shoulder. 'Plenty was, I knows fo' a
fac'. De kind ones was kind and de bad ones was bad.
But dey ain' no human, honey chile, got de right to own
no odder human. Caze men and women is men and
women in de eyes of de good Lawd.'

'All men born free and equal,' Richard said oratori-
cally.

'But — Moses? Where do you think he came from,
Granny?'

Granny shook her head. 'I ain' know. Not where de
mos' of 'm come from. Mammy say e stolen f'm e's
father. I ain' know where.' She leaned to take a nut
from the hot ashes and test it. The fire lighted her strong
brown face; lighted Lily's wide bright eyes.

'Git up, honey!' Granny told Lily, and herself rose
stiffly from her rocking-chair and went to a corner of her
room where a third stool stood in the shadows. She
returned, walking painfully, carrying the stool and holding
its age-dark top to the firelight while she scrutinized it
with eyes and fingers. 'Ain' hardly a mark lef',' she said.
'Pappy carve 'm when e set in de dark. E say Moses teach
'm.'

With a quick intake of breath Harriet tilted forward and peered. Richard was crouching beside Granny, his eyes puzzled.

'There's A and B and C; but theseyere don' look like no letters ever I've seen,' he said slowly.

'Richie, they — they look like —' Harriet began eagerly, only to break off. 'Granny, why do you kneel facing east when you pray? And why do you bow three times as you do?'

'Lawzy, honey chile!' Granny's voice was flustered, and she began over again. 'Lawzy, I ain' know why. Cep'n my mammy and my pappy done so befo' me, an' it seem like a proper kind of prayin'.'

Harriet's brilliant gaze went to the stool, with its tracery of characters half effaced by time, and to Richard's face, still bent above it.

'It must be Arabic!' she cried. 'And Black Moses must have been really an educated Mohammedan. Like that Ben Ali you read about, who left a diary in a desert dialect of Arabia. Oh, Richie, think of being a free Arab to start with and ending up as a Negro slave!'

'I don' quite make out,' Richard said, puzzled.

'Richie, haven't you read that chant, Allah il Allah il Allah — There is no God but God? That's how you began your prayer, wasn't it, Gran?'

'La-la-la-la-la!' Granny hummed acquiescently. 'I ain' know what it mean befo', but dat de blessed trufe. On'y one Lawd and E's Son, King Jesus,' she said reverently. She pulled the kettle to a cooler part of the fireplace and stirred it again, the warm peanut fragrance expanding through the cabin.

'A Mohammedan!' Harriet repeated musingly.

'And a good man dat was willin' to lay down e's life fo' e's frien',' said Granny.

'Listen!'

Through the still night came the throb of measured beating.

'De drum!' Granny explained it.

'Askin' folks to a Christmas week frolic,' Richard added. 'Granny, Harriet might hanker to go.'

The three 'chillen' ran to the door and stood listening to the exotic pulse in the blackness.

'I've read how they use a drum like that in Africa, to call people. What do they do at the frolic?'

'Oh, they march, and they dance — mos'ly square dancin' — an' they eat. Crowd the cabin so you cain' hardly move. They'll be another one tomorrow night likewise, sposen you like to go.'

'Maybe. But not tonight. It's more fun here. Let's sing, shall we?'

She laughed exultantly, and Richard and Lily joined her.

'We're lucky one way,' said Richard; 'we're such a laughin' people.'

'We're lucky anyway!' Harriet declared. She flung her head high. 'We have so much life in us. We can do anything we try to. Anything.'

XVII

THE CABIN IN THE CLEARING

RICHARD's mother had invited Granny and Harriet and Lily to New Year's supper. Harriet dreaded the event. There was no longer any strangeness in having Richard for a friend, when Richard was a lone figure, good and gay and gifted. But how would it be when she saw him in his own home, a part of a family?

His own home was beyond another cane patch and another thicket, and the guests arrived in midafternoon, in the sweetness of winter sunshine. Single file they entered the path that slanted off from the road. Lily led the way, her stockings drawn taut and her dress crackling with starch under her faded red sweater. She carried Granny Hayet Queener Sheber in both hands, straight in front of her, but her old root-doll, Rebecca-Rachel, was tucked under her patched red arm. Rebecca-Rachel had fine roots for hair and a rag-wrapped weed stem for a body; Granny had made her and dressed her.

Granny wore her best black dress, very ancient, with a beaded collar, and her snowiest headcloth and apron. Harriet followed them, a slim dark princess, with the warm fur of her coat collar and the rust-red of her hat framing her face.

Tall dry weeds closed in around them as they went: a forest of weeds meeting over their heads. The tallest were the wild beanies, the beans still rattling in their dry pods. To Harriet those tropic fugitives were part of Granny's story. She recognized the wild fennel, too, and the wild broom straw that made most of the island brooms. And here and there an okra plant, escaped from a garden, lifted exquisite late blossoms.

At the end of the path a round head dodged into sight, with another far below its level: dodged into sight; dodged out of sight again. Lily paused with a swish of skirts and a richly indulgent giggle. 'Aa'on an' Wash'ton!' she announced importantly. 'All bofe scairt of Hayet.'

Almost immediately, Richard was striding forward to meet them. He twitched one of Lily's braids and 'pulled his foot' in a bow to Granny, while his eyes went past them both with a questioning smile for Harriet. It was an anxious smile, as if he, too, had been wondering how his home would impress her. He backed against the wall of weeds with his arms outspread to hold them back, and let his guests pass him, Lily strutting ahead, into the Corwin clearing.

Harriet stopped short and looked. Like Jericho meeting-house, the cabin was enclosed in shadowy woods. A vast live-oak spread its arms behind and looked down, down, down on the pine-shake roof, caressing it with streamers of moss. The wind murmured high overhead as Harriet had heard it in Northern pine woods.

Before it the dooryard was swept clean as a floor, and a holly tree, bright with berries, adorned it. Harriet drew a deep breath. Here lived both peace and beauty. She smiled at Richard, who had stood anxiously watching her, and his face cleared.

'Not much like where you-all live,' he said. 'There's Mom, Harriet.'

The Cabin in the Clearing

The face he turned to his mother held no doubt, no apology. She came across the porch to greet them, round and warm-brown and comely. 'Y'all sho' welcome!' she cried. 'Us proud to see you, dis New Year Day.'

Little Washington nearly tripped them in his efforts to keep hidden in his mother's skirts, but they were all finally inside the cabin. There Aaron was grinning and pulling his foot and his forelock, and a ragged old man, wizened and dry as a cricket, bowed deeply to Granny. This was Grampa; not Richard's grandfather; just a grampa-in-general, who had dropped in to sit by the fire a while and eat when eating-time came.

Harriet studied the small sitting-room, while Richard took her hat and coat and hung them in a corner. One of the windows held a shining pane of glass; otherwise this was much like Granny's sitting-room. The bed was big and puffy; the walls and ceiling were covered with fresh layers of newspaper; the mantel was trimmed with cut-out scallops. On the mantel, beside the faded picture of a man whom Harriet guessed to be Richie's father, was a snapshot of Harriet, neatly framed in sand dollars. On the center table with the Bible was the book of American Cities.

'Mis' Corwin — Mis' Corwin!' Lily was saying breathlessly, holding Granny Hayet Queener Sheber high so that her hostess might appreciate its splendors.

'My land to goodness!' Mrs. Corwin exclaimed. She looked the doll's clothes over with interest while Washington tried to climb up her to see better and Aaron tried to see without appearing to. 'Who ever done make y'all sech gran' doll-baby clo'es?'

Lily thrust her thumb backward at Harriet and then plugged her mouth with it.

'E too pretty fuh break,' Mrs. Corwin said anxiously. 'Lemme set 'm on de mantelpiece, honey. Wash'ton jest raven fuh git 'm.'

'I got Rebecca-Rachel fuh play wid,' Lily agreed, and she nestled the root-baby in her arms and watched delightedly as Mrs. Corwin enthroned the queen in her knitted coat beside Harriet's picture.

Mrs. Corwin excused herself with bobbing bows and went back to see to her dinner. Pot lids clattered and whiffs of savory smell came through the open door. Granny laid off her voluminous old coat and sat down across the fire from the old man, and Lily ran out with Washington.

'I'll show you the yard if you don' mind, Harriet,' Richard said, and held the door for her to precede him.

The habitual forest twilight was deepening into an enchanted dusk. Killdeers called plaintively and frogs chorused. Silently Richard pointed through a shadowy vista that led to a dark gleam of water. Among the rushes a white crane poised on one leg like an ivory carving.

'It's so lovely — so lovely!' sighed Harriet.

Lily dashed around the corner of the cabin. 'Hayet!' she begged, 'come see de house me 'n' Wash'ton build yes'day.'

The young people followed her. They passed the big iron wash-kettles standing on their dead embers. They passed the pile of rice waiting to be thrashed with two rough sticks hinged with a bit of rope; waiting to be polished in a mortar that was a hollowed section of tree-trunk. They passed the brick well of the cane mill, with its long pole where the 'critter' was hitched to revolve the millstones. They passed the clean, tight chickenhouse. They came to the staggering playhouse, like an African hut with cornstalk corner posts and straw-thatched roof, where Washington sat in cherubic dignity.

It was all Harriet could do to keep from picking up the master of the house and hugging him. He was the kind of child who sets fingers itching to touch him. At three years he had not lost his baby plumpness. His mouth was a moist, carnelian-colored pucker, his eyes big and solemn and velvety, his little body as straight-limbed and dimpled as a cupid's.

Lily asked him, 'De baby wake?' and peered past him at Rebecca-Rachel lying on a straw pallet in the corner. With eyes watching Harriet for the effect of her house-keeping, she seized a little broom of wild bamboo and twigs and swept her dooryard vigorously.

'I'm so glad to have made your acquaintance, Mrs. ——' Harriet turned to Lily with exaggerated courtesy — 'Let's see: I didn't catch the name.'

Lily snickered behind her hands. 'Name Mis' Co'win. Dis Mist' Co'win. E my husban'. Git up, Wash'ton, and make yo' manners.'

The gentleman plunged forward on his dimpled brown hands and scrambled thence to his feet. He rolled his eyes up at Lily and made an obedient bow, flopping down on all fours again in the process.

Lily rescued him and brushed broom straw from his tight, black curls. 'E awful li'l,' she said dubiously. 'Y'all think e ketch up wid me?'

The visit was interrupted by a stifled shriek from the cabin door. It was a shriek of pure terror, and both young people went leaping toward Mrs. Corwin, who stood shrinking back from the step with Aaron peering over her shoulder.

When they came up she was pointing with a shaking finger at the step. A small object lay there, indistinct in the dusk. Richard leaned over and picked it up.

'Now-now, Mom,' he coaxed. 'Ain' nothin' but some fool chile flung it here to skeer us.'

He dangled the small bag with attempted nonchalance, but his mother only chattered with panic, and Grampa, looking over her other shoulder, showed the whites of his eyes in like fear.

'Listen, Mom,' Richard went on, 'I take it and drown it and that's all they is to it. Ain' nothin' — never was nothin' — sho' won' *be* nothin' oncet the water's drownded it.'

He loped away toward the rushy gleam Harriet had seen a few minutes before. She walked slowly after him and stood waiting for his return, herself too puzzled for words. He returned, rubbing his hands together, and grinned sheepishly.

'Some smart chillen,' he scolded. 'Like to scare Mom clean outen her wits.'

'But what on earth —— ?'

'Conjure bag,' he said briefly.

'*Conjure bag?*'

He nodded. 'Somebody puts roots and a lock of yo' hair in a little small bag and puts it where yo' bound to step over it. To put a charm on you; make you die or have bad luck.'

'Richard, you don't believe any such thing!'

He shook his head. 'Booker chillen learn better,' he said without full conviction. 'But Mom still thinks the old way.'

When they went in, they found Mrs. Corwin moving jerkily around the kitchen, picking things up and setting them down, her brown face still ashen. Granny was saying, 'Sho', Mis' Corwin, dem signs an' conjures don' have no power over no true believer.' Richard patted his mother's plump shoulder and added soothingly: 'It done drownded, Mom. Nothin' to fear.'

'Could I help, Mrs. Corwin?' Harriet asked. 'I'd love to.'

Mrs. Corwin looked at Harriet's glowing knitted dress, at her well-groomed hands. 'Y'all too fine, honey,' she

said, making a valiant effort at composure. 'Richie 'n'
Aa'on, dey he'ps me most as good as gal-chillen.'

Nevertheless, Harriet and Richard both tied on clean
aprons and helped set the table and dish up the food.
Granny gossiped with Grampa before the fire and the
children fell to playing again near them, still uneasy over
the grown folks' fright. Richard talked with determined
cheerfulness. He showed Harriet the stove he and Aaron
had got their mother, and explained how he meant to seal
the whole interior of the cabin with matched boards as
soon as he could afford to, so Mom wouldn't have the
bother of papering it every year. He intended to add
window sash, with glass, one at a time, too.

'Dat chile got highfalutin ideas,' his mother said quaver-
ingly, as she set a steaming dish on the table, but her
glance at her tall son was an admiring one, mingling dependent wonder and pride.

'Would y'all please to come to supper?' she called to
the old people, and they came with alacrity, Grampa
stepping stiffly like rusted machinery, but with a mass of
pleased wrinkles under his white thatch.

Dinner was good, with wild ducks that Richard had shot,
and liver pudding, and fruit cake richly flavored. Grampa
ate steadily but with an abstracted gaze.

'Mis' Freeman an' me wonders if it ain' dat no-count
Mis' Jones done you like dat,' he mumbled with his
mouth full.

'It was some no-count mischiev-i-ous chile!' Richard
said quickly. 'Grampa, we ain' gwine think no more
about it. They ain' no — any — magic anyway. Booker
teach us that.'

Grampa cackled, eating again as fast as his toothless
gums would allow. 'Might it was a chillen,' he conceded,
'caze yo' Mom ain' got no ill-wishers. But Booker don'
knows ev'ything. Whi' folks mebbe ain' need signs, but

de good Lawd gib 'em to colored. Colored folks ain' need book-learnin'.' He mumbled another delicately roasted morsel of duck, smackingly. 'Yo' Mom ain' need no receets fuh cook good. She ain' need no book-learnin' fuh raise three likely boy-chillen. Looka dat Wash'ton. Why e ain' puny an' crook-laig? Caze e mammy feed 'im pot liquor an' tie chicken bones round e neck so e don' suffer wid e teethin'.' He sucked the juicy flesh from a breast bone resoundingly.

The talk went on, talk about cooking and hunting and the white folks coming to the island for the winter season. White folks were so tender they couldn't come to their homes on the islands till after the hard frosts had set in.

Harriet sat looking at the delectable Washington, lost in thought. Pot liquor. That was the juices of boiled vegetables, rich in salts and vitamins. How recently the scientists had found out about those vitamins! How long the islanders had been making babies strong with them! But not all the islanders were wise, that was clear: too many of their babies had the bow legs, the winged shoulder blades, the large heads, of rickets; the span of life was still too short.

If you had sense, thought Harriet, you might get along pretty well without book-learning; but most folks didn't have that much sense.

Mrs. Corwin had sense; she was a fine person, even though she hadn't gone beyond the shanty schools. But her face was only now regaining its color, and Harriet felt very sure that it had required a heroic self-control for her to go on so quietly with the supper.

Granny and Aaron helped with the dishes. 'Y'all go 'long in an' make some music,' Mrs. Corwin bade Harriet and Richard.

So Richard made up the fire, with a polite word to Grampa, who was already nodding beside it, his sharp

chin with its grizzle of sparse beard resting on his collarless
shirt-front. Richard drew up a stool for Harriet, and took
down his banjo and plucked it, and they sang. Lily and
Washington were playing mysterious things on the floor
with Rebecca-Rachel and some jackstones.

How music made homes of the humblest places! Harriet
thought. She closed her eyes and tilted her head against
the newspapered wall and sang, and didn't know where
she was. She opened her eyes and watched Richard play,
his feet wrapped round the front legs of his stool, his head
on one side, his eyes dreamy and smiling. When both had
stopped, breathless, she reached out her hand for the
banjo.

'Y'all ever play one?' he asked, bringing the stool down
on its front legs with a thump and handing her the instru-
ment.

She shook her head, trying the banjo hesitantly. After a
few moments, guided by her knowledge of music in general,
she was plunking soft chords for one of the Landers songs.
It was a song that teased her memory with its simple words
and the haunting melody borrowed from an old spiritual.
She sang, and Richie hummed a deep accompaniment,
like bees in clover.

> 'Landers, Landers, Landers, Landers,
> I do love you for your name.
> Landers, Landers, Landers, Landers,
> I do love you for your fame.
> I would keep your banner,
> Ever keep your banner
> High!'

Richie's face was shining with happiness. He was looking toward the kitchen door, and Harriet turned and saw
that Mrs. Corwin and Granny stood watching and listening, and Aaron peered over his mother's head.

'Y'all see?' Richie demanded. 'This girl ain' white folks. No. I know she can make the piano holler for dear life; but she can take my old banjo, likewise, and make it sweet-talk as good as I can. She ain' too grand,' he finished simply.

Hurriedly Harriet started another tune, her cheeks burning.

They sang on, and presently they heard outside a strident, monstrous cough. Grinning, Richard strode to the door. 'Booker boy,' he explained. 'Got an old automobile. When we got gasoline, we ride all round Gentlemen's. — Please excuse me.'

He was back in two minutes, clearing his throat uncertainly. 'I told Sam you-all don' want to ride in any old car without springs and doors,' he said.

Harriet sprang to her feet. 'Oh, don't I?' she mocked. 'If Granny doesn't mind — At home we call them jaloppies, and lots of kids have them.'

'I like it, too,' Richard admitted.

Harriet looked respectfully to Granny for consent, and Granny nodded. 'Reckon young uns has to be young uns. Put on yo' hat, honey chile, likewise yo' coat. — No, Lily, Wash'ton ain' gwine, neider Aa'on.'

'Ain' any mo' room,' Richie told her gently.

The jaloppie was waiting in the road, one yellow eye glaring through the blackness. Sam hopped out from under the steering-wheel and shook hands with Harriet, and Richie helped her in.

'Got to git some water,' Sam said, and ran with banging pail to the pump.

'Radiator does leak so bad,' Richie explained.

Sam poured the water into the radiator, Harriet sniffing the sharp smell as it promptly began to leak out upon the dusty road. Then he found a place to hang the pail, and dashed to the front of the machine and threw himself upon the crank till the engine began to cough purposefully. He wriggled under the wheel again and the jaloppie gave a big hump and a big bump, and lurched sidewise over a stone and leaped ahead.

It was the jaloppiest jaloppie Harriet had ever met. Its seat-cushions were gone, so they must ride on bare boards. Its doors were missing, so that Richie braced his long legs, with the skill of custom, across the opening.

Harriet jerked her hat down tighter and wished she had a way of tying it under her chin. She began to laugh. Bump! and they would all leap upward together as if from a springboard. Thump! and they would all come down as if they were trying to break through the boards. Bang! and the only thing that kept them from flying out of the car was the tightness of the front seat.

'I'm s-sure g-g-glad there isn't any t-top!' she stuttered through her laughter. 'Our h-h-heads would go r-right through! — Oh, my hat!'

But Richie had caught her hat just as she felt the cool draft of its departure. He caught it with a convulsive swing of the hand that had been holding to the place where there wasn't any door.

She pulled it down as tight as she could. 'If I c-could only t-tie it!'

After another amazing contortion, Richie produced a folded handkerchief. 'T-try that!' he shouted above the roar and rattle.

Harriet put it on cornerwise over her small hat and managed to knot it under her chin. As they came into a band of light streaming from an open cabin door, she saw Richard studying the improvised headcloth with a queer smile.

The car banged to a stop and Sam was out, with his pail, and dashing to the pump, while the jaloppie stood shaking itself like a wet dog.

'Sam must have to take a regular route,' said Harriet, 'to be sure of water.'

'Ain' got to go far fo' water, not on Gentlemen's,' Richie reminded her. 'Harriet, is this too rough for you-all? Sure you don' want to go back home?'

Harriet chuckled. 'It's such fun you couldn't hire me to go home.'

It was a wild ride. Sam drove hunched forward with a heavy foot on the accelerator, and the car roared through the deep dust of the road, to the tune of loud explosions. It hit an occasional little board bridge with a jolt that jarred the words out of the riders' mouths and the breath out of their lungs. The one headlight picked out the weeds by the wayside, the tangles of palmetto and oak, the pickets of a fence. Beyond the margins of the road was nothing but deep black, except where light glimmered through the cracks of an infrequent cabin. The jaloppie seemed boring through limitless dark a tunnel lined with light.

Sometimes Sam flung himself at the wheel and wrenched the car to the side of the road to avoid a 'critter' placidly ruminating in the middle of the way. Often the darkness gave back paired green lights, high or low, that were the eyes of beasts, big or little. But they met no other head-lights: not a single car of any sort.

They did not try to talk much, for talking meant a stuttered shout. Once Sam, face straight ahead, did ask, 'G-girl name of C-c-countess at L-landers?' And Harriet shouted back, 'Y-yes! Y-you know h-her?' And Sam answered, 'M-met up with her oncet. — Wh-whyn't y-you bring her to G-gentlemen's sometime?' And Richie began to laugh. And Sam shouted, 'Aw, sh-sh-shut yo' mouth, Richie!' and laughed, too. He had a big, clean laugh like Richard's.

They laughed until Harriet could scarcely bear the ache

of it. And they sang funny tremolo songs. And then they jolted up a ridge of sand and stopped short.

'Who says I cain' turn on the moon?' Sam asked, out of a deep stillness.

There they sat, sole owners of those miles of beach, with the breakers booming softly and a glow deepening at the far horizon. Silently they watched as the glow sharpened to a keen red sickle, to a broad blade, to a semicircle, to a full round.

When it had really risen, so that its aching beauty and magic were dimmed and it no longer seemed profanity to speak or sing or laugh, Harriet softly sang 'Oh, Mammy Moon,' the boys bumbling along below her. Then, reluctantly, Sam backed down the sand ridge and maneuvered his way around into the road again, and they went bumping and snorting and galloping home.

It was not late when Richard and Harriet came, blown and laughing, into the Corwin cabin, but Lily and Washington lay sprawled asleep, the plump feather bed rising roundly about their small bodies. Old Grampa had gone, and Mrs. Corwin, placid again, was showing Granny her quilt pieces.

'Oh, Granny, we had the most fun. — And the moon! Richie, I didn't suppose Sam would be like that.'

'Like what, Harriet? Sam's kind of human.'

Harriet dropped down beside Granny to look at the quilt top spread out across her knees. It was a wonder of intricate piecing.

'Has the pattern got a name?'

'Sho' nuff: Star of Bethlehem,' Mrs. Corwin said, reaching over to smooth it fondly.

'Ain' — *haven*' we got plenty quilts, Mom? Why you want to wear out yo' eyes piecin' mo'?' Richard teased, standing with an elbow on the mantel, watching them, while the old hound nosed his hanging hand.

'Y'all knows good and well what disyere quilt fo',' Mrs. Corwin scolded. 'I sells chances and makes a heap of money on it.'

'Tell 'em what fo' you want the money, Mom,' Richard persisted.

'We gwine git us a Rose'wald School on Gentlemen's!' Mrs. Corwin explained. 'I ain' got no book-larnin' my-own se'f, but ——'

Her eyes went past Harriet to the bed and she heaved herself hastily to her feet.

'Hab mussy!' she went on, all in the same breath; 'efn dey ain' a hat on dat bed!'

While Harriet watched, open-mouthed, Richard picked her hat from where she had dropped it beside Lily. With his eyes twinkling, he took a pin from beneath his coat lapel, and gravely stuck it into the hat. His mother loosed a sigh of relief and then looked sheepishly at Harriet.

'Cain' learn me no diff'ent now,' she said. 'I done growed up on signs, seems like. — But I reckon de book-larnin's good fo' de young uns. I sho' be glad to God if Wash'ton grow up good as Richie an' Aa'on. So it look like I got to put in some heavy licks, workin' fo' de white folks' schoolin'.'

XVIII

Big Manor School

LETTERS awaited Harriet when she went back to school
after the short Christmas holiday. Among them was one
in Mrs. Trindle's finely formed writing. It said:

Dear Little Harrie:

Papa and I have been thinking of you so much the past
month. Your letters have been pretty cheerful, all but the
one in November after you had been over to Booker School.
But we are afraid that that one just showed what was in
your little heart all the time.

Yes, we do have a heavy burden in all the illiterates of
our race; but we have a good chance, too, if we will stand
up and face things.

However, Papa and I think you deserve the very best
opportunities you can have, and not to be crushed by too
much of a burden, either, especially while you are so young.

So we have been looking into the matter of your going to
that Charleston school this next semester. I know what
you're likely to say: that there is not enough money. If
there weren't, we'd be glad to help out; but with your little
annuity and the education insurance, you can make out,
by being very careful. A payment should be reaching you
within the week.

Then you can visit your great-grandmother, the dear old soul, in the summer, and return to us and your university course next fall.

When Harriet had read and re-read the letter, she tapped at Johnnie's door and showed it to her. Johnnie skimmed swiftly through it, and then sat gazing through the bright black slits of her eyes into a sassafras tree outside.

'It seems the sensible thing to do, doesn't it?' Harriet asked.

'Yes. Oh, yes, it does seem — sensible.'

'You don't know how let down and soothed I feel' — Harriet spoke with a vehement rush — 'and as if that old load had been dumped off my back.'

'You and Miss Joan both going —' Johnnie meditated aloud. 'Let's go tell Miss Joan, shan't we?'

Together they clattered down the stairs and over to the next hall, where Miss Joan and another of the younger teachers had two small bedrooms and a sitting-room.

'Sit down and make yourselves at home,' Miss Joan called from her bedroom. 'I've just come home from borrowing me a bathtub!'

'Won't you be tickled to death to get back to the kind of living you've been used to?' Johnnie asked.

'Mmmm! Tickled pink!' the young teacher gloated. 'Cold bath every morning, hot bath every noon, shower in betweentimes. Soft beds. And — hey! would you look at this!' She emerged in slip and robe, tragically holding out a silk dress spotted with mould. 'Just hanging in the closet! I found a pair of shoes ruined today.'

'My very best handbag has mould in all the creases. But what I hate more is having those silverfish sort of slither away every time you open a book. And I never had seen a cockroach before,' Harriet said meditatively. 'I caught one that measured four inches — including the feelers,' she added hastily.

'*She's* going away from here, too,' said Johnnie, kicking at Harriet.

'I'll read the letter to you while you finish,' Harriet offered. 'Shall I, Miss Joan?'

'It's the only thing to do. Isn't it?' she said, folding the letter when she had read it, and sticking it back in its envelope.

'What about your lessons with Magdalen Bates?' Miss Joan asked.

'She goes to Charleston once a week anyway,' Harriet reminded them. 'So that's as long as it is short. — Of course I'm going to miss the Negro History course with Miss Francis. I'll miss practically all the teachers. But ——'

'What about Granny's farm?' Johnnie inquired negligently.

Harriet felt suddenly empty. She hadn't yet stopped to think that Charleston would leave her no margin for saving that hundred or so dollars.

'I don't know why we should expect that that Northerner would push the matter now,' she said uncomfortably. 'Why would he, when he's let it slide eight years?' But I hope to goodness nobody will try to nab it for a truck garden! she was thinking miserably.

'Have you told Miss Francis?' Miss Joan asked, coming out and stooping to peer into a small mirror while she combed her damply curling corn-colored hair. 'It will make a vacancy for some other girl.'

'I'll — tell her.' Harriet went slowly over to the office.

Miss Francis took a long time to read the letter, while Harriet stood waiting in the shabby office, thinking that it would be only a half-year or so before she would be

free to enter beautiful up-to-date buildings again: adequate
buildings.

She read this year's Senior poster:

'Do you want something $\begin{cases} \text{made?} \\ \text{cleaned?} \\ \text{repaired?} \end{cases}$ Ask us!

Do you want Charm? Visit the Senior Beauty Salon!'

Miss Francis folded the letter and tapped the desk with
it, musingly. 'Won't you take a little time to think it
over?' she asked. 'Of course I see Mrs. Trindle's point;
but I don't believe you're wasting your time here, even
scholastically. Nor pining away with melancholy.'

Harriet shook a vehement head. 'No, but I do get
awfully depressed by the poverty and hopelessness.'

'You and Johnnie bring viewpoints that are fresh and
wholesome, now that you've adapted yourselves to the
situation. Please wait a few days before you decide.
And — Harriet!' she sent her clear low voice after the
departing girl, 'wouldn't you and Miss Joan like to go
with me on the semiannual visit to the rural schools this
week? Since neither of you will be here much longer you
might like the opportunity.'

Harriet regarded her suspiciously.

'The party always includes one or more students,'
Miss Francis went on with a flicker of amusement. 'I
think little Clapp wouldn't be bad: she comes from some-
where off in that direction. We'll go in on the main, to
Grand State, and Jerusalem; and maybe to Mossie's —
Big Manor, I think it is, though we've never been there.'
She pivoted her chair to look at the school schedule on the
wall. 'Friday. Meet here at eight-thirty.'

The first schoolhouse where they stopped that Friday
morning was Grand State, and it was a cabin on stilts with

a rickety pair of steps at its front door. As she approached those rickety steps, Miss Francis laid a finger to her lips and stood listening. The girls listened, too. Voices came unmuffled through the thin walls.

'Firs' three grades stan' up!' the teacher ordered. The consequent bumping and shuffling gradually subsided.

'Say yo' ABC's,' the teacher directed.

The voices responded in swelling chorus, some round with certainty, some ragged with doubt.

'Count to one hunderd!'

Again the voices obeyed, shouting at first and gradually waning to a murmur.

'Be seated!' said the teacher.

'Don't look so shocked,' Miss Francis murmured. 'What can you expect, with school only four months a year?'

She knocked at the door and introduced herself, and led the way inside, somewhat to the confusion of the teacher, since hers was the only chair and all the benches were filled.

The day was rainy and chill, and the wooden shutters had had to be closed, so that the schoolhouse was dim. Harriet peered around her, dodging a drip of rain through a hole in the roof. Fifty pairs of eyes turned as if by machinery from Miss Francis to Joan, to Harriet, to Mossie. Fifty pairs of feet scuffed or padded on the floor when fifty children rose and said, 'Good mo'nin', m'm!'

The smallest boy and girl could not have been more than five years old, and they were padded fat with clothes, like Chinese children. The little boy's stocking came rumpling down over his shoe, and the little girl straightened it with motherly pattings, and tied it with the twist of rag that was the garter, while he stared, uninterested in clothing, at the strangers. The biggest boys, in the back of the twilit room, looked sixteen or more. The whole fifty, five years old to sixteen, sat down, crowding the backless benches.

Covertly Harriet appraised the broken floor; the round red stove which made a hot ring of air around itself and then gave up the struggle; the patch of wall painted grayish black and serving as a blackboard. On it the teacher had lettered:

Time is To Costly Too Waste.

The teacher's homemade desk held a few ragged books and a cowbell. Hats and sweaters covered an end wall. A bucket of water and a dipper occupied one end of a rickety bench, and a huddle of paper lunch bags the other.

Miss Francis was telling about Landers. Joan told them a story, to which they listened open-mouthed. In conclusion Miss Francis beckoned the teacher to the door, and Harriet helped her lift a tied and labeled carton from the back seat. They drove on.

'What sort of things do you bring them?' Miss Joan asked.

'Oh — pencils, tablets, old readers from up North. And clothing, of course. One thing I wish we could get a lot of is United States maps. I wonder if one of the filling station companies wouldn't donate them. Just notice how few you see on the walls of these schools.'

'But — pencils and paper!' Pencils and paper had seemed to Harriet the irreducible minimum of equipment, taken for granted.

'Some of 'em chillen sho' be t'anksful fo' de clo'es,' Mossie observed. 'It awful col' dis time of year, gwine barefoot to school.' She wriggled her feet reminiscently.

The next schools they encountered were much like the first. Noon came, and the Landers party found a pump where they could wash their hands, and drew up beside the road to eat their lunch before they set out for the fourth school on their list.

'Now,' said Miss Francis, as they came out of that fourth school, 'we'll have to hurry if we hope to make Big Manor. We've never taken it in, because there aren't any real roads.'

'Big Manor my school,' said Mossie. 'I knows jest where e at. — On'y I don' know where's we!'

Following Mossie's wavering finger, Miss Francis drove off into the woods and stopped at the nearest cabin to call from the car. At her hail a woman peered through the window and ducked a bow and listened to her query. Her answer was fluent, but Miss Francis looked bewildered.

'Mossie, can you understand what she says?'

'Sho', m'm. E say we duh go long disyere road to de fo'k, an' den to de right twell we cross de track, an' den crost de field an' over de crick on de boa'd bridge an' crost anodder field an' through de crick; an' den we gots to walk a sma't piece twell we gits to de quarters an' den past de quarters twell we dere!'

The ride that followed was a strange one. The car sidled and creaked through stubble and ventured timidly on the two planks that formed the bridge — one for each pair of wheels. The four occupants heaved a fourfold sigh when it crossed with a final bang. It lurched through another field, straddling a faintly marked cart road. It dipped into another creek and splashed through it and reared up out of it. It settled down with a sigh and a shiver, and Miss Francis got out.

She hoisted out another carton, and the four took turns carrying it, two at a time, through a dry cottonfield.

'How much farther do you think, Mossie?' Miss Francis asked, easing her side of the burden down and wriggling her tired shoulders.

'Jest a li'l piece now, m'm,' Mossie answered, straining eagerly ahead.

It was really only a little piece to the quarters, a village of whitewashed cabins facing each other across a hard-trodden road. The quartette skirted its borders, seeing only an old man and an old woman, and a young man 'licking out rice.' All three bowed and grinned and called greetings and stood watching them as they went.

And then it was only another little piece to the school-house on the hill.

From the stovepipe a wisp of smoke trailed languidly. Mossie ran up the steps and pushed at the door.

'E gone home!' she wailed. 'Ain' nobody here!'

The others followed her in, the floor quaking so ominously under them that Harriet went flying, hop, skip, and jump, to avoid the most perilously teetering of the boards.

'Disyere where I mos'ly set,' Mossie told them, sliding along the handhewn bench to the window. 'So I could git out when ey fit. An' likewise so I could look outdo's.'

Harriet felt her throat tightening as she surveyed Big Manor. It was really the worst of the five. Planks nailed across the back corners of the room formed two of the seats. The window shutters creaked dismally. She could not see a single bright or lovely thing.

'But there is a map!' Miss Joan exclaimed, as if her thoughts had been following the same furrows. 'It's the second one I've found today.'

It was a packing company's map of the United States, and its dimensions were perhaps twelve by sixteen inches.

Harriet's gaze was pulled past it to a pair of eyes like brown and white agates in the back window. A small boy was hoisting himself up to the sill. He was a clean enough little boy, but his cumbersome trousers were held up by twisted strings tied to safety pins on his shoulders, and his feet were bare to the cold. His eyes were trained on

Miss Joan, in the most intent and astonished stare that Harriet could remember. When the young teacher smiled at him he dropped out of sight as if he had been shot.

Harriet turned around. A dozen youngsters were sitting quietly on the benches, and others were stealing in at the door on cautious tiptoe.

Miss Francis regarded their expectant faces, their hands spread primly on their knees.

'Where did you fall from?' she asked. 'Would you like to hear a story?'

'*Yes*, m'm!' they chorused after an instant's pause. '*Please*, m'm.'

'Harriet,' Miss Francis suggested, 'are you ready with a story?'

Harriet stood up and gathered her courage. At first her voice came thin and husky. 'I'm going to tell you about some Indian children,' she began. 'These Indian children are called Hopis and they live in Arizona.'

'Mmmmmm!' said the children in chorus.

Harriet stopped, rather taken aback. 'How many of you know where Arizona is?' she asked, trying to get her bearings.

Hands remained fixed on knees and eyes on Harriet. Two big boys in the back seat nudged each other.

'Will one of you point out your own state for me, on the map?'

A big boy raised his hand and shuffled up to the little map. Once there, however, he was lost. He looked at the north, at the east, at the west, at the south. He trailed a forlorn finger across the prairie states in the middle. He rolled eyes of dumb appeal at Harriet.

Coloring hotly, she pointed to South Carolina, and to Arizona, straight across from it. Then she began her story:

'Once upon a time, long ago, the Indians in Arizona were fighting with the Mexicans just south of them ——'

'Mmmmmm!'

'— and one of the Indians found a little Mexican baby boy that had been left behind on the trail when his parents were running away ——'

'Mmmmmm!'

Now it was Harriet who cast a look of appeal, and at Miss Francis. Miss Francis looked as astonished as Harriet was feeling. There was nothing to do but labor on, though she found herself hurrying when it was time for that periodic response. All the children, even down to the smallest, gave her the most painful attention. The boy who could not locate his own state watched her and listened with alert interest. The teacher, informed of their coming, stood by the door and listened almost as eagerly as the pupils.

When Harriet had finished, dizzy and out of breath, Miss Francis said: 'One of your own old neighbors is with us today: Mossie Clapp. She has been in Landers only a few months, but she is doing well. Mossie, don't you want to tell them something you've learned at your new school?'

Mossie, too, had known that this request was coming, yet her face went gray with fright as she stood clutching the desk.

'I — maybe tell 'm what ey should eat for breakfast, an' how fuh set de table.'

Miss Francis nodded, and Mossie addressed herself to her principal, as if there were no one else in the room. She told Miss Francis that she should have cocoa and hominy grits and milk, and that she should use oilcloth on the table, or else a tablecloth — 'flou' sacks makes good tablecloths' — and put the plates and cups and spoons on just so, and sit down together — 'stead of grab yo' food like dogs an' run wid it,' she reproved Miss Francis.

She concluded with eloquence, undisturbed by the

regular chorus of 'mmmmm's.' Shifting her eyes for one instant to a small boy, she demanded, 'Wha' y'all had fuh breakfas', Frankie?'

Frankie rose, thrusting out his small stomach self-importantly. 'Coffee 'n' hawgmeat,' he announced.

'You-all tell yo' mammy give you cocoa an' grits an' milk an' make you strong chile!' Mossie adjured Miss Francis, and sat down, quivering with fear and triumph.

Her talk had been a copy of one of the school nurse's. The pupils had watched her with wonder — Mossie Clapp, very spruce in her second sewing-class dress, a red and white checked gingham with red revers and red buttons on its double-breasted blouse. Her looks, from the red ribbon drawn through her rolled hair to her black oxfords and red-striped anklets, spoke much louder than words. They even drew attention somewhat from Miss Francis and Miss Joan, who had apparently made such a sensation. When Miss Francis had dismissed the postscript school, it clustered around Mossie. The smallest girl went around behind her, as if to make sure that the glory was not all in front, like a paper doll.

Harriet sat very still as they rode toward home. 'You know,' she exploded at last, 'I wouldn't have believed there were such schools in the United States.'

'This particular school has one unusual feature,' Miss Francis said mildly. 'Some of the children have never seen white people before.'

Miss Joan gasped and sputtered. 'But Miss Francis —! Will you say that again? You don't mean —? Why, how many miles is it from the highway?'

'I know; but I do mean it. It's true, isn't it, Mossie?'

'Yes, m'm. Dey plenty dem chillen ain' saw no whi' folks twell dis wery day.'

'But — how could that *be?*' Harriet demanded.

'Mostly the lack of roads, I suppose. No roads to

bring the white people in and nothing to take the colored people out. — I know it's almost unbelievable. But the whole school situation is pretty hard to believe. The last statistics I've seen showed that our state spent an average of $7.84 per colored child per year for education. Some counties spend less than that.'

Harriet gulped. 'What is the average for the whole country?'

'I don't know exactly. Somewhere under a hundred dollars.'

'How can they expect us to rise when we've no more chance than that?'

'And the mountain white schools aren't a bit better than Big Manor, either,' Miss Joan commented.

'Whi' folks' schools? Sho' nuff?' Mossie's face was pure amazement.

'It's the whole South that's suffered, these seventy-five years,' Miss Francis observed. 'Not just one class: Negroes, rich whites, poor whites.'

'I often wonder what became of — of our white people,' Harriet said slowly. 'The Taliaferros.'

Mossie listening hard, as she still must to follow this unfamiliar tongue, gasped and rolled her eyes at Harriet. 'Tollivers? Ey live in house ain' far f'm Tolliver Plantation,' she said. 'Efn y'all take de nex' turnin' ——'

Harriet clasped her hands hard. 'Would it be too far out of our way, Miss Francis?'

Miss Francis glanced at her watch. 'It might not be a bad idea,' she said.

Between swamps where the frogs sang eerily, past little gray church houses staggering on stilts, past the crossroads store — 'Datdere's Tolliver's!' announced Mossie, who had sat well forward in the back seat, directing.

Miss Francis slowed the car. 'Would you like to get out and see Mrs. Taliaferro, Harriet?'

Harriet frowned earnestly. 'Yes, Miss Francis, I think I really would.'

A very small Negro girl answered the jangle of the old-fashioned bell and ushered them into the chilly, high-ceilinged parlor. Silently she scurried to call her mistress, and presently Mrs. Taliaferro came in, a little girl clinging to her skirts and whimpering to be carried.

Miss Francis introduced herself with the calm that was a part of her poise. She never needed vivacity for emphasis. Her quiet was emphasis in itself. 'And these two Landers students,' she said, 'wished to greet you because their ancestors served yours on Taliaferro Plantation.'

Harriet had risen at once, as she had been taught to do when an older person entered the room; and Mossie had slid off the edge of her chair and was busily making herself small.

Mrs. Taliaferro sat down and waved a hand toward the sagging mahogany sofa. 'I'm glad to make your acquaintance, Miss ——,' she said to Miss Francis. 'Y'all are Maum Clapp's little grand, aren't you?' she asked Mossie with mild interest. 'But the other one — she isn't a Clapp? — Hush, Betty!' The fair-haired little thing was whimpering and shivering.

'No, Mrs. Taliaferro. I'm Harriet Freeman, and I've been living in Minneapolis.'

'Freeman? — Freeman? — Betty, run and tell Lishy to make a fire if you're that cold.'

'Black Moses Freeman ——' Harriet said tentatively.

Mrs. Taliaferro raised her eyebrows and nodded. 'I've heard them speak of Black Moses. He was a smart darky, Grandmother Taliaferro always said.'

Harriet steeled herself to ask a question. 'Did you ever hear where he came from? What he was? They say he was educated in his own language.'

Mrs. Taliaferro said politely: 'But you know there were

so many such stories. This one was a chief or a king, and that one was a great warrior. But they all look pretty much alike now, don't they? — Black Moses was smart, though; I've heard that.'

The child pattered in behind small brown Lishy, who trailed splinters and chips after her as she came, her big eyes solemn above her double armload. Betty ran to Mossie's beckoning hands. Mossie was not shy with white babies. She had had much to do with them before she moved to the vicinity of Big Manor School.

'Such a lovely child!' Miss Francis commented, rising to go.

The mother rested a slender hand on the foam of blond curls. 'If she didn't have so much malaria,' she said anxiously.

'Wouldn't it be better for her up North?' Harriet inquired with her intense frown. 'I never heard of malaria in Minnesota.'

'Mistah Taliaferro's business interests,' the young mother replied vaguely. 'Must you-all go? Do come back again some day.'

Lishy opened the door for them, ragged shoes slapping scarred floor, and they crossed the porch, avoiding the missing board.

In the car again, no one spoke until they were bowling along the road toward the causeway. Then Harriet said, '*Worse!*'

Mossie gawped. Miss Joan looked inquiring. Miss Francis smiled at the narrowing road.

'They have a worse time of it than we do, those Southern white people who were used to being rich,' Harriet explained. 'That little girl — she looks poorly nourished, and she's chockful of malaria. And even the mother is sort of trapped.'

'What a wise young thing you're getting to be,' Miss

Francis observed in her light, level voice. 'Did you ever hear the characterization of Charleston: "Too poor to paint and too proud to whitewash"?'

'You mean,' Miss Joan interpreted, 'that they're bound by their past glories?'

'Won't do what they can because they can't do what they want to!' said Harriet. 'Oh, Miss Francis, everything about the North makes it easier to break loose and go ahead there!'

'Yes,' said Miss Joan, 'and today has made my decision for me. I'm going to teach in the mountain school.'

Again the three listeners reacted in three ways. Harriet folded her lips resentfully tight. Mossie's face was a complete blank: everything these outlanders did was mysterious. Only Miss Francis looked both comprehending and content.

'Well,' Harriet declared at length, 'I'm going to begin packing, myself. That's what *I'm* going to do.'

XIX

THE MAJESTY OF MOSES

SATURDAY was too busy a day for packing or even for
planning. Sunday morning found the girls walking into
town to church in a long queue of galoshes and raincoats
and rain caps. Sunday afternoon was calling time.

During dinner the rain stopped. Patches of robin's egg
blue showed through the gray clouds. When the sun
glinted out, a thousand diamonds quivered on tall grasses
and long mosses. Birds went wild with song. Girls broke
into gay little runs as they crossed the campus to their
dormitories.

For Sunday afternoon was calling time.

From two to six the girls were permitted callers: 'home
folks,' 'boy friends.' With a teacher acting as hostess,
they gathered in the big living-rooms of Sarah B. Soon
little girls, too small to have callers, would come scurrying
to knock at dormitory doors and say, 'Deena May, young
man askin' for you-all' — 'Roseanne, yo' folks is here,' —
'Le Misher, you've got a caller.' Sad the hearts of those to
whom no messenger came; loud and defiant their laughter
together, or else frank their tears.

All along Harriet's corridor girls were primping. They

dashed into and out of each other's rooms with brief preliminary taps.

'Deena May, you-all gwine wear those blue beads? Mind if I borrow 'em?'

'Le Misher, cain' you tie my hair bow like yours?'

'Got any high-brown powder, chile? Somebody spilt mine.'

'Which you reckon looks best: this dress or this?'

Harriet pulled off her checked taffeta and pulled on a brown wool skirt and a furry orange sweater. She was changing her silk stockings for smart thin wool when Mossie came racing down the corridor.

'Hayet!' she gasped, 'Pearlie Randall say tell y'all you gots a caller. Big tall one. Reckon it dat Richie?'

Harriet puckered her brows. 'You don't suppose anything's the matter with Granny?' She thumped into her brown and tan oxfords, knotted the ties with swift fingers, and ran down the stairs and over to Sarah B.

Already the big rooms milled with young people. There were big country boys, ill at ease among all these dressed up and chattering girls, and their girls as ill at ease as they; two young sailors from a naval base not far away, their round dark heads rising cockily from precisely creased blue collars. There was Richard, sitting somewhat self-conscious in a straight chair, watching the door.

Harriet thought it was nice to see him spring up at sight of her; nice to see him 'pull his foot' in his old-fashioned bow, when she introduced him to Miss Francis. He was much nicer than any of the other boys gathered in clusters throughout the room.

The two young people wove their way toward a pair of chairs in a far corner. Progress was slow. Willie Lou accosted them with a shout: 'Hattie, meet my friend Georgie Clarke!' Round little Phyllodoxia, all aglow, lisped: 'Oh, Harriet, my brother from Atlanta Univer-

thity! Thith ith Paul, Harriet.' Roseanne did not stop
them; she stood aloof with her handsome mother — the
woman Harriet had met at Landers entrance the first day
— and drooped scornfully amused eyes at the others.

When at length they reached their safe haven, Richard
was breathing convulsively, as if he had been swimming a
stormy sea.

'It was so nice of you to come!' Harriet said. 'This is
probably my last Sunday at Landers. Next week I was
coming over to see Granny. And then — Charleston!'

Richard seemed scarcely to hear her. 'Harriet,' he broke
in, 'we been having tur'ble lot of this flu sickness break
out on Gentlemen's.'

'*Granny?*'

He nodded. 'She's bad sick. Mom's been doing what
she could, but — well, you saw how it was: Mom don'
know the new ways.'

'*I* know them. — How soon can we get a boat?'

'Efn we make haste ——' Richard was on his feet and
Harriet weaving through the throng again, this time blind
and deaf to salutations.

She told Miss Francis of Richard's errand, and received
permission to go to Granny at once. While Richard
roved round the campus, she threw together the clothes
she thought she should need; found the treasurer and from
her obtained money for the boat trip and for supplies she
would get at the Bosquet drugstore. She silently gave
thanks that the instalment of her annuity had come the
day before — a money order, cashed and deposited with
the treasurer. Checks were of little use here, as no banks
had survived the depression. She was rather glad she was
not tempted by checks: it was so easy to write too many
of them, and she must use as little money as possible. The
trip to Charleston, tuition, books — these would strain
her resources.

By this time Miss Joan had learned of the emergency and backed out her car to take the young people to town and to the boat. All the way Harriet was ticking off lists of supplies on her fingers.

'A hot-water bottle — Granny wouldn't have a hot-water bottle, would she, Richie?'

Richard looked blank.

'A rubber bag to put hot water in to keep on their lungs or wherever there's an ache,' she explained.

'We use a hot brick. Or a bag of hot salt.'

'And just as well, too,' the teacher commented.

'We-ell. Mentholatum to rub on her chest.'

'Ain' lard 'n' turkentine good enough?'

'We-ell. Plenty of oranges and lemons to make fruit juices for her to drink ——'

'Granny's got plenty oranges from her own tree.'

Even in her anxiety Harriet laughed. 'And of course she has mustard, for mustard poultices.'

'You might take some canned things for yourself, and canned soups to feed Granny when she can eat them,' Miss Joan suggested. 'And some changes of sheets. — It's Sunday, but maybe I can coax a storekeeper to break into his store for us.'

By their combined efforts they had the revised list of necessities all together in time for Harriet and Richard to run, panting, upon the boat just before it tooted and frothed away from the dock. They stood and waved at Miss Joan until she turned back to her car, and then they settled down in Harriet's favorite bow seat.

'Now!' said Harriet. 'Richie, how long has Granny been in bed?'

'Ain' been in bed till day befo' yesterday,' he told her. 'Been a-coughin' round for a week — ever since y'all went back to Landers, I reckon. But now she's a sight worse. Fair burnin' up with fever.'

Harriet smote her knee. 'I should have got a thermometer!'

'Cabin's nice and tight,' Richard objected. 'Got plenty of wood to keep it warm.'

'Thermometer for Granny's fever,' she explained.

'So now Granny an' Lily are both two in bed,' he went on after a puzzled pause.

'Have they had the doctor?'

'Ain' no doctor on Gentlemen's.'

'Well!' Harriet ejaculated; 'thank goodness I've had courses in the care of the sick. And thank goodness I had influenza last winter, so I know the best ways of taking care of it. Probably I can get her well in time so I won't have to be much late for Charleston. I'm **sure** Miss Francis will let me make up this week's exams.'

Richard crossed and uncrossed his knees and laced his long fingers over them. He looked through his lashes at Harriet, the brightly expectant look of one who springs a delightful surprise. 'Like enough I'll be seein' y'all in Charleston.'

'What do you mean, Richie?'

He grinned. 'We just got it fixed up. Jick did.'

'Jick?' she asked, her mouth wry as if the name tasted unpleasant.

'Jick's smart, Harriet. He even got the truck painted up fine and marked "Cotton-Blossom Kids."'

'*Cotton-Blossom Kids?*'

'Yes, m'm. "Cotton-Blossom Kids. Jazz Orchestra and Quartet." That's me and Jick and two other chillen. One boy, he tap dances like a hen on a hot griddle and all the time lookin' like he's clean out of his head with joy. Me an' Jick, we play the banjo and the other boy's got a sax; and we all sing good. — We're gwine shoot straight for Charleston while the white folks are there from up No'th; and when we've got all the loose money in Charleston, we're gwine on up along the coast. Maybe, like y'all say, we make a big hit in Harlem.'

He stopped, eager for applause, but Harriet's mouth was tight and her brows were twisted. 'Oh, Richie!' she flared, 'do **you** think you'll like anything so — so —— ?'

He stared at her, crestfallen, and she shook her head and flung out her hands.

'What about the work you're planning here, Richard? What about helping your people redeem their little farms?'

'Reckon it's too late to help them thataway,' he said soberly. 'Another fellow's been around lookin' 'em over, studyin' to buy 'em up to raise garden stuff. — And if it ain' too late, I got mo' chance to help by earnin' money — seems like. Besides seein' the world the way y'all said, Harriet.'

'But the work — the *work!* Don't you remember what Miss Locke told us that day —— ?' Her voice dwindled. After all, how could she object? She who had roused his ambition for travel in the first place? She wriggled around on the bow seat, with her back to him and her foot tucked under her and going to sleep. 'I've got to try to think what I'll do first for Granny,' she said ungraciously. Her eyes stung with tears, and she kept her head turned away: her nose got lavender-colored when she cried.

Heat a sack of salt — in a covered spider in the ashes? Give Granny a sponge bath to make her more comfortable — she should have got bathing alcohol!

(What a contrast, Richie standing by the sea like a statue of young Moses, planning the deliverance of his people, and Richie in candy-striped trousers and a tilted hat, playing jazz for dimes!)

Squeeze oranges and give Granny the juice ——

(Richard might get the taste for that dusty excitement; might keep on with that sort of life! And she had loved to hear him say, 'my people.')

Clean the cabin and air it ——

(How cheap a calling seemed if it had no real service in it. She shook her shoulders and covertly wiped her eyes and nose.)

Almost before the boat had docked, Richie was helping her down the gangplank, and they were clattering over the loose boards of the pier and loping through the dust. Harriet had never yet felt it necessary to 'walk like a lady' when haste was needed. She carried her parcels and Richard her suitcase, and the greater weight handicapped him just enough to keep his pace equal to hers.

He grinned at her as he stretched out a long arm and opened Granny's gate; an anxious grin, like a whipped puppy's overtures of friendship. 'We — run — good together!' he panted.

Harriet didn't smile back. She gave him a swift, frowning glance and clattered across the porch and into the cabin.

Granny sat straight up in bed, burning eyes on the incomer. 'Chile of Moses!' she said in a cracked, husky voice. 'I pray de good Lawd an' E sen' me de chile of Moses!'

'Hayet, e do talk so funny!' wailed Lily, rolling over against the girl and hiding her hot little face in Harriet's cool coat. 'I skeered.'

But Granny had lain down, long dark hands crossed on tumbled counterpane. 'Chile of Moses — An' 'im flogged to deaf fo' e's people. Flogged twell e done dead ——'

Harriet flashed a startled look at Richard.

'Yes. I done hear that, likewise. Granny wouldn' have told you if she had her wits. — Flogged to death caze he taught them to read and write. — Don' take shame, Harriet. Don' take shame, honey.'

Harriet's head went up. 'Shame? I'm proud as the dickens.'

'RICHARD, SHE REALLY IS BETTER'

The Majesty of Moses

She had no time to stop and meditate on a martyr forebear. 'Richie, would you build up the fire and get fresh water? And then stay out a little while?'

Harriet had learned the technique of bathing the sick and putting fresh linen on the sickbed, but she had had a doll for the patient. She was hot and breathless and aching of back by the time she had two live patients cool and fresh between clean sheets.

Granny went on talking, talking, gazing with uncanny eyes at the rafters. Occasionally she sang.

Richard knocked diffidently.

'Come in,' Harriet invited from the stool where she had dropped. 'Excuse the mess.' She nodded toward the sheets and pillow cases she had piled in a corner. 'As soon as I catch my breath I must sweep the dust out from under the bed. Queer. It's clean everywhere else but there.'

Richard twisted his cap. 'My people think it's a bad luck thing to sweep under sick folks' bed. Kill 'em sho'. — Or to wash their face, either.'

'Was the piece of rag tied around their front hair one of the old ways, too?' she asked. 'Lily's was pulled so tight her eyebrows were screwed up into the middle of her forehead.'

'Yes, m'm. It's s'posed to hol' up the palate and cure the sore throat and the cough.' He grinned uncertainly, and they laughed together, more at ease again after the stiffness that had lain upon them.

But the laughter roused Granny, who had lain quite still, her lips moving as she picked at the knot of a comfort. She sat up again. 'Ain' not'in' — fuh laugh about!' she protested. 'Ain' not'in' — not'in' — not'in' ——'

Gently Harriet urged her back on the pillow. 'There, Granny. Lie still and Harriet'll make you some orange juice. And in a little while you'll be all well again — all well again.'

Granny gazed at her soberly, rationally. 'No. Ain' gwine git well no mo'. De good Lawd gwine fetch me home. — White man come projeckin' roun' after dis li'l ol' farm. Gwine buy it up fo' de taxes. Say I got to git out dis spring.'

The hoarse voice creaked to silence, while the two young people stared at each other and Lily stared from them to Granny, nodding affrightedly and whispering, 'Hayet, yes, m'm, white man did say thataway.'

Again the old woman opened her parched mouth, speaking painfully. 'Ain' never gwine leave dis place cep'n to go to Heaben.'

Harriet and Richard tiptoed out to the kitchen and Harriet began to squeeze the oranges Richard had brought in and heaped on the table. 'You think that's really so?' she asked in a dry voice.

'Reckon so, Harriet.'

Tight-lipped, she carried a jelly glass of juice to Granny and one to Lily, who smacked eager lips over it. Then she filled a kettle with water and dropped in a spoonful of healing benzoin and set it in the fire so that it should send its steam into the room.

Meanwhile Richard went home and changed to work clothes. When he came back to milk the cow he brought a covered bucket with hoecake and rice and a crisply fried fish for Harriet. By the light of the log fire she ate hungrily, and Richard sat back on his heels and watched her.

'Have you eaten anything?' she remembered to ask.

'No, not yet. Reckon I got to be gettin' along. But, Harriet, if you need Mom, either me, you just toot Granny's old horn, will you?'

Richard did not even get out of the yard. Harriet had buttoned the back door and gone in to Granny's bedside, feeling small and young and fearful, when a hoarse shout from Granny herself brought him running back. Lily launched herself upon him, terrified, as soon as he stepped into the room.

For Granny was sitting up again, brandishing her arms and gasping on the top of her shallow breathing: 'Gwine home! Gwine home! Look away yander, chillen; buckruh done come a'ready to run po' Granny off. E cain' come. E cain' come!'

Wildly she clung to Harriet, staring over the girl's shoulder at the darkest corner. Her old face writhed with fear and sorrow.

And then Harriet spoke, steadily. 'He isn't coming, Granny. He isn't coming, ever. Harriet's going to keep your little farm safe for you.'

The old woman listened, and her frightened eyes turned to the girl's face, searchingly. Frowningly serious, that face; calm and sure Harriet's voice.

'First thing tomorrow Richie's going to Bosquet and get Harriet's money for her,' the girl went on, soothingly. 'And pay the taxes. And then the place will be yours for good and all. You'll go for us, won't you, Richie?'

Richard nodded. 'Sho' will,' he said dazedly. 'Do anything for you-all, Harriet. — Either Granny.'

Granny's eyes still searched her grandchild's face. 'You-all got de cash-money?' she quavered.

Harriet swallowed hard and nodded. 'Sho'!' she said emphatically: and did not even notice how she had said it.

Quite suddenly and simply, Granny curled down in her bed and slept.

Richard stood tall and somber with his arm on the mantel and looked down at Harriet, rocking in Granny's old chair, a quilt-wrapped bundle that was Lily filling her arms. Lily had crept over and climbed up into Harriet's lap, pleadingly silent as a puppy.

'Y'all mean it, sho' nuff?' Richard asked. 'About the money and buyin' back the place?'

'Do you think I'd have said it if I hadn't meant it?'
Harriet rocked harder and then stopped because a board
creaked too loudly. 'I'll write a note to Miss Francis.
She'll understand.'

'But — does it leave you enough fuh go to Charleston?'
She shook her head.

'But ——'

'I don't *want* to go to Charleston. I — I want to finish
at Landers. Afterward I'll go somewhere not too far
away — maybe Spelman, in Atlanta — where I can learn
lots more about Home Ec — nursing, cooking, diet,
babies. And then' — her voice thickened with earnest-
ness — 'I'm coming back to Gentlemen's and help my
people *live*.'

'Harriet, *your music?*'

'Oh, I'd keep up my music, every way I could.' She
laughed out suddenly. 'Wouldn't a Steinway look funny
here? We'd all have to move out.'

'It ain' no joke, honey. *Common* folks could teach my
people ——'

Harriet didn't protest that she was common folks.
Maybe the common folks weren't common, either: but
she knew *she* wasn't. She felt bigness, sureness, strength,
within her.

'What I really want is to compose, Richie. Music, you
know. You reckon I'd do more if I was in big cities,
whirled around and gay? No. I'll do bigger things on
Gentlemen's. I know it.'

Granny turned and muttered, and Richard was beside
her in one stride, a firm hand on her head to quiet
her.

'Harriet,' he asked, 'ain' it a good sign when they begin
to sweat?'

Harriet rose and thrust Lily into his arms. Eagerly
she bent above the bed, laying her palms against Granny's

neck, listening to her breathing. 'Richard, she really is better. — I'll fix another salt bag ——'

Richard laid Lily on the bed and went after more wood. When he had finished making up the night's fire, he straightened, dusting his hands, and looked at Harriet, a long, wondering look. 'You mean it, sho' nuff. — Comin' back to Gentlemen's.'

'It took me so long to see it.' Harriet spoke in a vehement soft rush, while she adjusted the salt bag and poulticed Granny with brown paper buttered with lard and turpentine as Richard had advised. 'But it's the most wonderful chance to do something — big! I might have to teach a while, to earn a living. But I'm young. There's time. And I'd get my people working for a Rosenwald school, like your mother, and' — She let out a long breath and looked at him shiningly. A cricket chirped loud and near and again they heard the reiterant chorus of frogs, the sigh of the wind, high in the trees, as if it had mysteries and wisdoms beyond mortal knowing. 'Such a place to make music, Richie! Such a place! And likely I could go away often enough so I'd love to come back — so I'd always know how beautiful it is.'

'Chillen, cain' y'all sing sump'n' fo' Granny?' The deep old voice came suddenly, quietly. 'Seem lak I kin sleep good efn y'all sings.'

They sat on the old handhewn stools on each side of the fire and Richard began, his voice big and sweet:

> 'Great Day,
> The righteous marchin'——'

Harriet sang, too, gazing deep in the fire. From one song to another they passed, before Richard, tiptoeing to the bedside, lifted a long finger. 'Bofe two asleep! Reckon I gots to go, Harriet.'

'Richard! You haven't had a bite of supper!'

He shrugged careless shoulders, as if his mind were on matters far from food. But he did not go.

'My people are so stubborn,' he warned her. 'It ain' gwine be no easy work, Harriet.'

'Don't I know it?' She struck her hands together. 'What do I want of easy work? I'm strong enough for hard. If Black Moses could die for my people, I guess I can work for them.'

'I thought you'd be shamed,' Richard muttered. 'Y'all thought he was king-proud — Black Moses — and him flogged like a horse.'

Still her eyes shone in the firelight. 'It took just that to make me see. — Only I can't teach them to farm their tracts so they won't lose them,' she conceded, her triumphant voice flagging, 'or grow good cattle or build good houses.'

A pocket of resin bubbled and spat on the fire. A shutter banged. A cricket chirped and the wind was still. The cat rubbed its arched back silkily against Richard's big shoe. Granny was breathing in deep, quiet rhythm.

'That will have to be somebody else,' Harriet said wistfully.

'*Me*,' said Richard.

He flung his arms wide, and his face, with its dark planes sharp-cut by the firelight, held the leader look she had seen before. Then it relaxed, and his teeth flashed white.

'Girl,' he said, 'it's gwine be fun, likewise!'

THE END